"I think it's time for some on-the-spot research," Jake said

His kiss was hot and demanding. Julia trembled with arousal. *She wanted him.* She had to get away—now—before she gave in to desire.

"Jake, uh, Sheriff . . ."

"You're not interested in continuing our research, Dr. Shelton?" he asked teasingly. "Maybe the porch isn't the place. Inside, then?"

"It's not the time or the place, Sheriff." She moved his hand from her shoulder. "My work is important, and I'm certainly not going to bed with the opposition."

"Who said anything about *bed?*" Jake said, oh-so-innocently. "There's a nice sofa in the den. There's a great big kitchen table. . . ."

She pushed him away. Hard. He grinned roguishly and gave a little shrug. "Whatever you say, Doc. But there will be other moonlit nights, and we'll share one of them soon. I guarantee it."

Dear Reader,

Temptation is Harlequin's boldest, most sensuous romance series . . . a series for the 1990s! Fast-paced, humorous, adventurous, these stories are about men and women falling in love—and making the ultimate commitment.

January 1992 marked the debut of Rebels & Rogues, our yearlong salute to the Temptation hero. In these twelve exciting books—one a month—by popular authors, including Jayne Ann Krentz, Barbara Delinsky and JoAnn Ross, you'll meet men like Josh—who swore *never* to play the hero. Matt—a hard man to forget . . . an even *harder* man not to love. Cameron—a rogue *not* of this world. And Jake—he *never* backed down from a challenge.

Twelve rebels and rogues—men who are rough around the edges, but incredibly sexy. Men full of charm, yet ready to fight for the love of a very special woman. . . .

I hope you enjoy Rebels & Rogues, plus all the other terrific Temptation novels coming in 1992!

Warm regards,

Birgit Davis-Todd
Senior Editor

P.S. We love to hear from our readers!

The Wolf

MADELINE HARPER

Harlequin Books

TORONTO • NEW YORK • LONDON
AMSTERDAM • PARIS • SYDNEY • HAMBURG
STOCKHOLM • ATHENS • TOKYO • MILAN
MADRID • WARSAW • BUDAPEST • AUCKLAND

To Dominique Mondoulet-Wise,
for her support and inspiration

Published April 1992

ISBN 0-373-25489-X

THE WOLF

Prologue

JAKE FORRESTER stepped into the air-conditioned lobby of the Cattlemen's Club, handed his wide-brimmed Stetson to the hatcheck girl and headed toward the dining room.

Fred Gilmer was already seated and wasted no time getting down to business. "There's a dame out at the old Farrell place," he said irreverently as soon as Jake joined him. "One of those educated types, a doctor of something or other. Anyhow, I hear she's a looker."

Jake had heard the same rumor. He waited.

"But that's not what interests me at the moment, Jake, although it might interest you."

Jake raised an eyebrow but didn't comment. He was used to being needled about his success with good-looking women.

"Fact is, you're the perfect one to check her out, you being the sheriff and the sort of handsome guy who just might get this gal's attention."

Jake ran a hand through his Stetson-rumpled hair. "Is this your reason for inviting me to lunch, Fred?"

"You could say so." Fred leaned back in the large chair. A few years older than Jake, he lived what was considered the good life in Pierson County, New Mexico, and it showed in his heavy build and ruddy complexion, Jake reflected.

"Discussion before lunch or after?" he asked.

"Before, but *during* drinks. Linda, honey, come on over here," Fred called.

The fringes on Linda's short leather skirt and halter top fluttered as she sauntered over to their table. "Sure, Mr. Gilmer." She looked at Jake.

"Haven't seen you in here for a while, Sheriff."

"Been busy, Linda. Keeping Pierson County safe for lovely ladies like you," Jake teased.

Linda smiled. "Well, don't stay away so long next time. Drink orders, gentlemen?"

"Bourbon and branch for me. What about you, Jake?"

"The usual," Jake replied easily. "Club soda with a twist."

"I'll be right back."

Both men watched Linda's retreating figure with approval. "Now there's someone who makes leather look good," Jake said.

"She does, indeed." Gilmer was thoughtful for a moment, then spoke quietly, "Doesn't it get old, Jake, the club soda routine?"

"Old?" Jake laughed. "Let's just say it never gets any easier. That's the bad news. The good news is that I don't think about it so much anymore, except maybe at times like this. Right now I'd like nothing better than a cold beer."

"Well, my hat's off to you for staying on the wagon all this time."

"I take it from day to day, Fred. That's the only way."

Linda arrived with their drinks and took their lunch orders.

"Old times," Fred said, raising his glass.

Jake touched his glass to Fred's. "Now, what the hell is this all about?"

"Before I answer that, I've got a question for you, Jake. What do you know about the Farrell spread?"

"It was just bought for a university project. They've posted a large tract for wildlife research, I believe."

Fred smiled. "You do your homework, old buddy."

Jake shrugged. "Keeps me out of trouble."

"You've done a damned good job since we put you in office."

"Breaking up a fight or two on Saturday nights and handing out an occasional speeding ticket?"

"There's more to it than that. We count on you to keep an eye on what's happening, and you haven't let us down."

"Let's say I have plenty of time to check things out," Jake replied. "Now, what's the problem at the Farrell place?"

"From what I'm hearing, that so-called wildlife research is led by the gal I mentioned. And it could be detrimental to the ranchers and the county." Fred shifted in his chair and took a cigar from his breast pocket, rolling it slowly between thumb and forefinger. "I'd appreciate it if you'd just mosey out there and lay down some guidelines the Cattlemen's Association put together."

Jake's interest was piqued. If the Cattlemen's Association was involved, whatever was happening at the Farrell place could be very important. The C.A. was the most influential group around.

"Sounds interesting," he commented lazily.

"I'll tell you confidentially, Jake—" Fred leaned closer "—what's happening out at that old ranch could cause us all a hell of a lot of trouble one day."

1

JULIA SHELTON watched from the window of the adobe house. A car was coming down the dirt road, traveling fast, the roar of the engine cutting through the peace and quiet. It was an unwelcome intrusion.

She went to the door, shielding her eyes against the glare of the afternoon sun. The desert shimmered in the spring air and the sky was a cloudless, blue expanse. It was a beautiful day.

She stepped onto the porch as the black and white Jeep screeched to a halt, a cloud of dust rising in its wake. The driver swung down. He was wearing a khaki uniform, sunglasses and a wide-brimmed hat. He approached her with an easy, almost lazy stride, obviously not in a hurry now that he'd set his black boots upon solid ground.

He stopped in front of her and pushed back his hat. As he removed his glasses, the lenses reflected the sunlight into Julia's eyes and he appeared for a moment to be surrounded by a halo. But Julia had the distinct impression that this man was no angel. He was far too handsome and sexy for that.

"Howdy, ma'am, I'm Jake Forrester, sheriff of Pierson County."

Howdy, ma'am! Julia tried not to smile. His words reminded her of scenes from bad cowboy movies. She extended her hand.

"Hello, Sheriff. I'm Julia Shelton. Is there some kind of problem?" She was sure that there couldn't be, not so soon. The university experiment had only just begun. Her tracking equipment was in place, and her assistant was in the desert, ready to release the wolves.

"No, ma'am, there's no trouble," he said with a hint of a drawl.

Julia breathed a sigh of relief. Everything could proceed as planned, and the team that had worked so hard to prepare the Mexican brown wolves for this moment of freedom could turn the project over to her.

Then she realized that the sheriff was still holding her hand. His grip was hard and strong. She took a good look at him.

She had to admit that she liked what she saw. The sheriff was in his late thirties, and he was lean and imposing, well over six feet. He would tower over her own five feet four inches. His tan only accentuated his green eyes, and deep laugh lines were etched at the corners of his mouth. Julia's gaze met his and the intelligence and awareness she saw in those eyes contrasted markedly with his laid-back speech and walk.

"No trouble at all," he repeated; he dropped her hand and stepped back. If Julia's scrutiny bothered him, he certainly didn't show it. He smiled as if asking if she liked what she saw. The smile was really something, a mixture of little-boy wickedness and sexy assurance.

Julia imagined that he was well aware of its effectiveness. His uniform was crisp, the boots highly polished under a faint dusting of desert sand.

She caught the tangy scent of his after-shave. The way he was looking at her suddenly made Julia acutely aware of her own appearance—disheveled hair, T-shirt dusty from moving furniture—and no makeup.

She pushed a wayward curl behind her ear. "Then I guess you're the official welcoming party." Before he could answer, she suggested firmly, "And please don't call me ma'am. I'm Julia."

"Well, howdy, Julia. I'm Jake." He'd avoided the *ma'am* this time. Jake stepped up beside her onto the porch and looked out across the desert's gently rolling hills. The scrubby growth was just turning green. "Lonesome out here, isn't it?"

"I like it," Julia answered. She did. A biologist and naturalist, she'd spent plenty of time alone in the wilderness and had always preferred those periods to her stints at the university. This was the perfect place for her latest project, which promised to be the most exhilarating and most difficult of her career.

"It's peaceful," she continued, "and very pretty now with the desert flowers blooming."

"You've only been here a few days," Jake pointed out. "Just wait a while."

"I always try to see the positive side," she said, trying to convince herself of the honesty of her words. Julia looked around at the adobe house that would be her office and home for the coming year. "Now that you're here, come on in and let me give you a tour of the facilities. I assume you know what's going on."

"I know a little," he admitted.

"Come on, Sheriff, I bet you know a lot. Otherwise you wouldn't be out here, checking on me and my wolves." She led the way into the house.

Her wolves. Jake stifled a grin as he followed her. Dr. Julia Shelton was sharp—sharp-tongued, too—and was obviously very proprietary about those wolves.

Before taking this trip to the Farrell spread, Jake had made it his job to gather some facts. Julia was in charge of a university project to return a pack of wolves, raised in captivity, to the wild. He'd expected that the professor running the project would be intelligent—also much older and much, much less attractive. He'd imagined that Fred's comment that she was a "looker" had simply been thrown in as an inducement. He'd been wrong.

Not that Julia was breathtaking. In fact, she was nowhere near as beautiful as some of the women he'd known in the past, yet there was something damn appealing about her. He figured that she had to be about thirty. It was hard to say; there was an air of vulnerability about her that she tried to hide with her brashness. He liked the way she met his gaze, direct and unflinching. He also liked the reddish tint of her curly chestnut hair, and her trim, well curved shape. Perfect.

Julia first took him through the living room, then down the hallway to another big room. "We've turned this into the office and tracking station," she explained. "The leaders, or alpha wolves, will be wearing transmitters, and when we tune in on their frequencies we can follow their movements." She pointed to a large map mounted on the wall.

When Julia flicked a few computer switches, lights glowed on the screen and the machine beeped reassuringly. Jake pretended interest in the display, which evidently fascinated Julia. He was certainly fascinated by her.

"Our equipment is state-of-the-art," she informed him. "The university paid a pretty penny for it, but this project is worth it." She hit a few more keys in her enthusiasm. "The wolves haven't been released in signal range yet, so I really have nothing to show you," she went on, reluctantly exiting from the program.

Jake shook off his fascination with the woman and forced himself to ask a question about her work. "Wolves. Why the hell wolves?"

She looked up at him. "And why not wolves?"

That was obviously all the answer he was going to get. They walked on, through the dining room and into the kitchen.

"Rather ancient stove but a great new fridge," Julia commented as she opened it and glanced at Jake. "Beer, cola, iced tea? Probably no beer since you're an officer of the law and on duty."

"No beer," he affirmed. "But iced tea sounds good."

"To me, too."

Jake watched while she got glasses out of a cupboard and filled them with ice cubes. Her movements were clean, efficient, without any wasted motion. She didn't even seem to notice his scrutiny, just went about her work. There was nothing flirtatious about Julia, Jake observed, but he was finding her very provocative, nonetheless.

She handed him the glass, and he leaned back against the sink and took a long swig. The tea was icy cold and refreshing. "So this is it? The whole house?" He knew it wasn't and wanted to see where she lived. A woman's bedroom could be very revealing.

"You're still interested? Okay." Julia walked out of the kitchen without waiting for an answer. He followed her down the hallway again, past a cozy den with a fireplace to her bedroom.

Jake scanned the room quickly. The walls were white, and the only pieces of furniture were a simple wooden bed covered with a bright Mexican spread in blues, greens and yellows, and a wooden dresser with a mirror above it. Colorful woven rugs were scattered across the wide-plank floor. He noticed there were none of the usual bottles of cosmetics or perfumes on top of the dresser, just a brush, lipstick and comb. He was intrigued.

Julia opened the dark wooden shutters and let in a flood of sunlight.

"Nice, but a little monastic," Jake commented.

"I find it comfortable and quite suitable for me." She smiled sweetly.

He nodded and looked around the room again. An image of Julia wearing a filmy black negligee flashed into his mind. He wondered if she owned anything like that. She probably didn't, he decided, but she was having quite an effect on him. His imagination was going wild within a few minutes of meeting her.

Julia walked past him, back down the hallway. "The bathroom's here," she said, pointing to a closed door, "there's a storeroom at the end of the hall, and here we are back at the den."

Jake walked into the cool room and dropped into a comfortable-looking chair. He wasn't ready to leave yet. He definitely was attracted to Julia, but it was time to get back on track.

"So why wolves?"

"It's a long story, Sheriff, one I won't bore you with now, but the short version is that wolves are marvelous creatures. They're highly intelligent and they have a wonderful social and family system. Perhaps more to the point, they were once an integral part of the ecological system in this area. Until man appeared."

"Snake in the Garden of Eden again?" He said it jokingly, but Julia remained serious.

"It's a familiar story, isn't it? When ranchers moved in, the wolf was hunted almost to extinction. There are projects like ours in a number of countries that have been preserving the species in captivity, but that's not where they belong. We're going to get them back into their natural habitat."

As she talked, Jake realized that he'd been wrong about Julia. She *was* beautiful, her blue eyes alight with excitement as she spoke. He was glad Fred had sent him out here to meet her. She was becoming more and more interesting.

Julia was still talking about her wolves, and Jake tried again to look interested. Finally she caught herself in midsentence and stopped. "I'm sorry. I tend to get carried away when I talk about the project."

"Please don't apologize. It's important to you, and it's nice to see someone who cares so much. Not many people do." Jake thought about himself, wondering how long it had been since he'd cared about anything.

She took a chair opposite him. "I need to learn not to lecture, don't I?" she asked, running her fingers through her hair. As soon as she smoothed her curls, they sprang up again.

Jake noticed that her movement was natural and unstudied. She hadn't meant to be sensual. Yet he was possessed by the strongest urge to reach out and touch her hair. He could easily imagine its silky texture beneath his fingers.

He studied her face closely as she began speaking again. Her nose was small and straight, and she had a provocatively kissable mouth. He tried to drag his mind back to her explanation but couldn't stop looking at her lips, wondering what it would be like to kiss her. How could he shift the conversation from wolves to more personal matters? Like a date.

"It's been a five-year battle to get this off the ground," she was saying, "but with a great deal of help, we've succeeded."

"I don't imagine that everyone is as positive about this project as you are," he responded. It was time to ease into his reason for being there. He already knew that Julia was too strong-willed to accept an ultimatum from the Cattlemen's Association gracefully, so he would have to approach the subject as obliquely as possible. Then, after their business was finished, he'd see how she felt about dinner.

"Of course not. Lots of people don't understand at all." She looked directly at him. "That might include you."

Jake finished his tea and set the glass down. There was nothing oblique about Julia.

"I like to keep an open mind, but as you guessed, my visit isn't purely social."

Julia leaned forward and replied calmly, "I know."

"What else do you know?" This sure as hell wasn't a woman who played games.

"I know that you're here to check me out, see what I'm up to," she said matter-of-factly.

"Right again." He had to smile. "And?" He paused, waiting for her to continue.

"No," she stated flatly. "You tell me."

Jake leaned back, took a deep breath and plunged into his explanation. "Some of the local cattlemen are worried about wolves coming back on the range."

She shrugged dismissively. "Believe me, they'd have more to fear from their family pets. The wolves have been in captivity and they'll have to learn first how to readjust to the wild."

"And then?"

"Most of them couldn't kill a cow if their lives depended on it." For once she hadn't answered directly.

"Even a calf?"

"Our wolves will be out on the desert on our own land, and they'll be more interested in eating rabbits, birds and gophers than raiding herds of cattle. Besides, they won't be anywhere near the ranches." She spoke very confidently.

"The ranchers are worried," Jake said, playing devil's advocate. "They won't do anything to hinder your project, as long as the wolves stay within the designated territory. But if the wolves kill any cattle, well, I imagine the ranchers won't stand idly by."

He didn't imagine it; he knew it damned well.

Julia's cheeks were flushed now. "I'm not sure I understand your role, Sheriff. Wouldn't your job be to protect me if the ranchers retaliate in some way against me . . . or the wolves?"

The question seemed innocent, but there was an edge to her voice.

"My job is not to take sides, but to uphold the law and keep trouble from happening." Jake knew his answer sounded glib.

"Then my wolves and I will just have to obey the law, won't we?" Julia retorted angrily and walked out of the den. His interview was over. He'd destroyed any chance of inviting this intriguing woman to dinner. Or maybe not. He'd have to look for another opening. Jake followed Julia into the living room. She turned to face him.

"Please tell the cattlemen that I appreciate their concern, but resent their warning. I also resent it that they sent you out here to tell me. There are other ways to handle a situation like this one. They didn't need to call the sheriff. After all, the project is still in the formative stages, and no law has been violated that I'm aware of." She looked at him challengingly. "Am I right?"

"As I said, it's my job. I like things to run smoothly here in Pierson County, ma'am." For some perverse reason, he'd deliberately used that word again. "I think it's best that all of us understand each other from the beginning."

"Oh, I understand perfectly," Julia retorted. "You and the Cattlemen's Association don't want anyone shaking up the status quo. Newcomers mind your manners, isn't that it? Well, I can assure you, Sheriff, that there'll be no problems from this end."

"I'm counting on that," Jake said.

She crossed the room and stepped onto the porch. He followed.

"But if problems arise out here—problems of any kind—remember that I'm always available," he added. "I hope you'll call on me to help."

She smiled, and Jake thought her anger had begun to fade. He decided it was now or never. "Maybe we could talk this over in a more social situation," he offered. "How about letting me buy you dinner tonight?"

"Do you always combine business with pleasure?" The casual question sounded innocent enough.

"When the company is as charming as you." Jake regretted his quick answer instantly. Julia frowned.

"I'm afraid I'll have to decline, Sheriff."

It was a definite *no*, and Jake was surprised; he was rarely turned down.

"Even though," she continued, "I imagine your friends in the Cattlemen's Association would like you to keep me in line twenty-four hours a day."

"I wouldn't mind that myself." Jake couldn't resist flirting even though he was on dangerous ground.

"Well, it isn't going to happen. Frankly, I'd feel as though I was fraternizing with the enemy." She crossed her arms.

"Now, ma'am." He hadn't meant to say it that time; it just came out. "I'm not your enemy," he protested.

"Oh, yes, you are," she countered fiercely. "You said you were just doing your job, but I expect your friends' concerns weigh a hell of a lot heavier than mine. To tell the truth, Sheriff, despite your charming and very calculated invitation for dinner, I don't feel at all welcome in Pierson County right now."

Jake chuckled. "I didn't expect such a strong reaction. It was only an invitation to dinner, ma'am. Fact is, I was trying to be neighborly."

Julia didn't bother to answer. She stood there glaring at him.

"Well," he said, putting his hat and sunglasses on, "it's a small county populationwise, anyway. We'll probably run into each other again."

"Until then, Sheriff. And thanks for dropping by. It certainly has been educational."

She hadn't even tried to conceal her sarcasm. Jake touched two fingers to the brim of his hat. "For me, too. Until next time."

"Goodbye, Sheriff."

There was nothing for him to do but leave.

As Jake turned the Jeep toward the highway, he looked into the rearview mirror. Julia was still standing in front of the adobe house, hands on hips, watching. He smiled. It *was* a small county, and he would see her again. So he'd struck out this time, but there'd be others. He liked her; he liked her spunk and the way she'd stood up to him. Not many women did that.

Of course, getting involved with Julia could complicate things if there was trouble with the wolves, but that was unlikely. Besides, he wasn't talking a serious relationship; that wasn't part of his life-style. But for now, Julia Shelton looked immensely appealing.

JULIA STOOD ON THE PORCH until the plume of dust stirred up by Jake's Jeep dissipated in the breeze. The visit had been more disturbing than she'd let on. She didn't like the idea that the Cattlemen's Association was already checking up on her even before the wolves had been released.

She turned to go back into the house, disconcerted, unsatisfied, and wishing that the visit with Forrester had gone better. She hadn't meant to lose her temper, but it was quite obvious that the sheriff was only interested in what the ranchers wanted. His interest in the wolves was nil.

Besides that, he'd been deliberately trying to handle her, to dazzle her with his considerable charm and good looks. She didn't like the idea that he'd been sent to spy on her.

She paused halfway up the steps. She'd handled their confrontation all wrong. It might have been best to accept Jake's invitation to dinner. She could have found out a little more about the politics of Pierson County, just who exactly wanted her watched.

Julia shrugged, recalling the times her grandmother had told her she could catch more flies with honey than with vinegar—a lesson that, no matter how she tried, Julia had never learned.

AN HOUR LATER, Julia was sitting at her desk, a pile of reports stacked in front of her. She hadn't been able to concentrate, and it was all because of *him*.

He was handsome, all right, Sheriff Jake Forrester. And he knew it. He'd just been doing what came naturally when he'd flirted with her, asked her to dinner. In spite of her grandmother's advice, Julia knew she'd made the right decision. Now she could work on the reports.

Her pep talk failed. Her mind kept wandering back to images of Jake walking lazily up the porch steps, leaning against the kitchen counter, lounging comfortably in the big den chair. Then she remembered what he'd said after perusing her bedroom with a glint of laughter in his eyes. He'd called it monastic.

"Well, my bedroom is none of your business, Jake Forrester," she said. "And I'm not going to think about you anymore today."

With that she mustered her thoughts and turned back to the reports on the sex life and mating patterns of the Mexican brown wolves.

2

JULIA WAS THINKING about the sheriff again. That didn't please her; in fact, she felt disloyal. She'd come out here to the Farrell house for a reason, an important one. The project was her main concern and she didn't want distractions.

She'd gotten up before daylight, started coffee brewing and headed for the computer in the office. She stared at the screen and dismissed Jake from her thoughts. The wolves had been put into position during the night, and the moment she'd been planning for was finally here. She typed in several commands and was able to locate their signals. Excited, she watched the blips that indicated their location move across the screen.

That was a first for her. *Her* wolves signaling from the desert, their lights glowing, almost as if they were speaking to her. *Her* wolves, free, in the wild again.

Julia smiled, exhilarated. She'd expected a little more activity the first time she picked up the signals, but of course she wouldn't find that now, not in daylight. This was their time for rest. She'd have to wait until tonight, when they would begin to prowl in their new territory. Rafael Santana would arrive soon to tell her all about the wolves' first hours in the wild, and she wanted to hear every detail. She pored over the project reports while she waited, keeping an eye on the terminal.

Yet when she heard the sound of an approaching vehicle, Julia's first thought was not that her assistant was bringing news of the wolves, but that the sheriff had returned. Only when the rumble grew louder, noisier than the well-tuned purr of the sheriff's four-wheel drive, did Julia realize it was Rafael.

Exuberant, she rushed to the front porch to greet Rafe with a big hug. Dragging him by the hand into the office, she began asking questions immediately.

"Tell me, Rafe, how did it go? Were they disoriented? Did they—?"

Rafael laughed. "Give me a chance to answer, Julia," he begged. "But first, how about a cup of coffee?"

"Oh, Rafe, I'm sorry!" She hurried to the coffee maker against the wall.

They settled down with their coffee in front of the terminal, and Julia repeated her question. "How did it go?"

"So far, so good," the young man replied. "They're resting now."

"I know. I can see that on the screen. Come on, Rafe," Julia said eagerly.

"All right," he agreed. "I'll start at the beginning. They *were* a little disoriented when we released them, especially the young ones, but we expected that."

"Yes." Julia nodded.

"The leaders were steady. Alpha One and Two headed straight for an outcropping of boulders and low scrub where they holed up. They were scared, but there was no disorder. They kept the pack together. They're damned smart, Julia."

"Of course. They're wolves." Julia was relieved that all seemed well.

"They're *our* wolves, which makes them unusually smart."

"Have they eaten?" She knew she sounded like a worried mother; it was exactly the way she felt.

"Some time before midnight they found the road kills we left, shot full of vitamins and antibiotics. They wolfed them down, so to speak."

Julia grinned. "That's a good sign, but they'll need help with food until they can hunt on their own." *Until*, not *if*. Julia was determined to be positive.

"Sure, that's the plan. There's a good supply of wildlife out there—gophers, field mice, rabbits. They shouldn't have any problems."

Julia avoided mentioning that the wolves' hunting instincts might have been dulled by captivity or even bred out of them. Rafe knew that as well as she; besides, other animals had returned to the wild and learned to feed themselves. These wolves would, too.

"Don't fret, boss." Rafe must have noticed her moment of doubt. "The older wolves had some hunting experience back at the compound. They can handle it. Besides, gophers aren't exactly known for their brains."

"Just keep the faith, eh?" she asked. She appreciated his reassurance.

"Hey, we're not going to let them starve, so relax. You should be proud of our success so far. You got the whole thing off the ground and operative."

"With still a long way to go."

"True, but we'll get there." His dark eyes sparkled and his handsome face broke into a smile. Julia thought how lucky she was to have Rafe on her team. He balanced her seriousness perfectly with his optimism and sense of humor. He was also ambitious.

The first in his large Mexican-American family to go to college, Rafe had grown up just a few miles from where they'd set up the tracking station. His parents and many of his brothers and sisters still lived in the area. Now, with a degree in biology and two years working on the project, he'd come home.

Julia had chosen Rafe for the field job, both because of his exceptional understanding of wolves in the wild and for his familiarity with the area they'd chosen for their experiment. He also knew the residents well.

Julia was reminded again of yesterday's visitor. "Jake Forrester stopped by," she said casually.

"Oh, the sheriff. Was it a friendly visit, or are we in trouble already?"

"On the surface he was friendly and quite charming," Julia responded, sipping her coffee thoughtfully, "but he was here as an unofficial official, I think. If you know what I mean."

"I know exactly. He's a good-looking dude, or at least the ladies think so. My mom is one of his biggest fans.

You should see the way she flirts when Forrester drops by the store."

Julia tried to suppress a grin and failed.

"Hard to imagine, huh?"

Julia knew Rafe's mom, and thinking of the lovely but motherly Pilar Santana flirting with Jake *was* amusing. "I'm sure they both handled themselves with aplomb and style," she told Rafe.

"On Mom's part, anyway. I'm not so sure about the sheriff," he added enigmatically. "I am sure, however, that he came out *here* for a reason. Remember, it's a small town, Julia. You'll have to get used to everyone wanting to know your business."

Julia got up and brought over the coffeepot, but knew she was being more than accommodating. She was buying herself a little time to think about what Rafe had said. He was right, of course.

"Yes, the sheriff had a reason. He was checking us out," she said. "He admitted it. He was also here to give me a kind of, well, I guess 'warning' is the best word."

Rafe glanced at the monitor; the wolves were still quiet. He got up, took their coffee cups and nodded toward the front door. "Let's sit out on the porch steps. It's looking like a beautiful day."

They sat on the steps and watched the sun as it climbed above the horizon, turning the desert to gold, lightening the dark sky to blue. A soft breeze wafted across the sand, ruffling the dusty scrub.

Rafe sat quietly for a few minutes, and then asked, "Just what was the warning he gave?"

"Implied, I should have said."

"Did it sound like a threat?"

"No, not really. It was a kind of friendly reminder that the Cattlemen's Association is watching and that we should keep an eye on our wolves. As if we wouldn't."

"And as if our wolves were a threat," Rafe added. "They should see them now, cowering under the rocks, afraid of their own shadows, not ready to catch a desert mouse, much less a gopher."

"I tried to explain that."

"Those guys are from the old school," Rafe said seriously. "They're descendants of the ranchers who hunted the wolves out of existence. I'd call anything that comes from them a threat."

"Even if it comes by way of the sheriff?"

Rafe nodded. "Probably. They're suspicious of anyone not born in their beloved Pierson County."

Julia nodded, thinking about the sheriff. She remembered the way he'd gotten out of the Jeep and walked toward her. The easy gait was certainly the manner of the West. So were his soft, slow drawl and the lazy half smile. But there was something else, something she couldn't put her finger on, that told her Jake Forrester hadn't spent his entire life in this part of the world. He'd been around, and not just around New Mexico.

"I don't believe Jake Forrester was born here," she mused.

"You're right. He's a relative newcomer."

"But they're not suspicious of him?" she asked.

"He had a sponsor in Fred Gilmer."

She repeated the name. "Fred Gilmer. Biggest cattleman in the area, president of the association."

"You've done your homework," Rafe said. "Nothing happens in this county without Fred knowing about it. I imagine he's the one who sent Jake out here."

"What did you mean when you said he was Jake's sponsor?"

"Apparently their friendship goes way back to Vietnam. After Forrester got out of the army he became a private detective."

"Not here?"

Rafe laughed. "No, in Los Angeles or some big city." He was vague. "I'd already gone off to school when he came to Pierson City. I've just picked up bits and pieces from my family."

"Gilmer brought him here to be the sheriff?"

"So it seems," Rafe replied.

"And the sheriff is Gilmer's boy?"

Rafe shrugged. "I'm not sure. That could be a little harsh, but I imagine Gilmer knew that the sheriff was paying you a visit."

"So," Julia observed, "everyone in town does what Fred Gilmer asks."

Rafe shrugged again.

"What about you, Rafe?"

He smiled wryly. "My association with Fred Gilmer hasn't exactly been pleasant."

"You left here at eighteen to go to college. What kind of trouble could a teenager have gotten into with Gilmer?"

"He has a daughter."

"Oh." Julia smiled.

But Rafe clearly wasn't amused. "Her name is Beth," he said a little bitterly. "We were friends in high school. Good friends. Gilmer didn't like that at all. We had a few run-ins."

"Oh," Julia said, but without amusement this time. This was going to be interesting. The most powerful man in the county didn't want the wolves—*and* he had a vendetta against her assistant. "Where is Beth now?" she asked, trying to keep her concern from her voice.

"Don't worry. I haven't seen her in years. She went back East to some fancy school, and I doubt if she'll be returning to Pierson County."

"You returned," Julia said pointedly.

"Only to help on this project." Rafe put down his cup and glanced at his watch. "And I'd better get with it. I need to take a reading on their location and then start tracking with the binoculars, if I can spot them." He stood up and stretched. He was only a few inches taller than Julia. "What are your plans for today?"

"Get organized," she replied. "That includes finishing my paperwork and trying to translate your field-note hieroglyphics into something readable. Then I need to take the car into town and have the battery checked. I've been having problems starting in the mornings."

"Want me to give you a lift home later? I can pick you up at the garage."

Julia shook her head. "I doubt if it'll take very long."

SHE HAD MISCALCULATED.

"Looks like it's the alternator," the mechanic told her. "Should be able to get to it by tomorrow afternoon."

"Tomorrow?" Julia was dismayed.

"Yep." The reply was accompanied by an apologetic grin that indicated it couldn't be helped. He offered to have someone drive Julia home, but she declined. There wouldn't be any problem getting a ride, she assured him as she started down the street.

The townspeople all seemed to live within a few blocks of Pierson City's Main Street, and Julia felt the same sense of "Hometown" she'd felt the first time she'd come here. On foot it was even more discernible.

It was warm and dusty. Apparently there had been very little rainfall during the winter, and the spring had come without much promise of relief. The heat was dry, not sticky, and the air was crisp and clean. The mountains in the distance showed off their verdant green to the barren valley below.

Julia strolled along, taking her time. She'd find a ride home easily; she wasn't in a hurry. The wolves would be sedentary for a few more hours, and she had caught up on her paperwork—except for deciphering Rafe's report.

Julia's conscience was just beginning to nag at her about that waiting work when she passed the Santana grocery store, but she decided to take a little more time for a chat with Rafe's mother. In the two weeks since Julia and Rafe had set up the tracking station, Pilar Santana had seen more of Julia than of her son, who'd been transporting the animals from the university holding pens to the desert.

"*¡Hola!*" Pilar said as she came out from the back room to greet Julia with a hug. "I have lost a son, as they say, but perhaps I have found a daughter."

"Rafe will be around more when the wolves begin to adapt," Julia promised.

"I hope," Pilar replied. "I had expected when he came to work on the project we would have him home again, but so far, he sleeps here only."

"So far," Julia repeated. "Give us time. I promise you'll have your son back."

Pilar laughed good-naturedly. "At least he is in the county, and for that we can thank you, Julia."

"I believe the thanks go way back, to you and Rafe's dad for giving him the education he needed for this job."

Pilar nodded. "And to my boy for taking advantage of it," she added proudly. "He is a good worker. *¿Es verdad?*"

"The best. And the smartest, even though his handwriting is from another planet. You have every reason to be proud."

Pilar chuckled. "His teachers always complained about the writing."

"And overlooked it just as I do?"

"I'm afraid so, which is why it never improved."

"Well, once I learn his strange alphabet, we'll be in business, and if the project survives, much of the credit will be due to Rafe's work with the wolves."

"He talks of nothing else when we do see him, but he brings no pictures of them."

"Pictures?"

"Yes, so we can see for ourselves these beautiful creatures he brags so much about. It has been many years since there were wolves in the wild."

Julia remembered packing a few snapshots she'd taken during the research stage. "I have some pictures at the tracking station of Rafe working with the wolves. I'll bring them next time."

"And maybe there will be some of the wolves in their new home?"

Julia shook her head. "The idea is for them to get far away from humans and to learn to fear them. That's their only chance for survival. Later we may get some aerial photographs, but not yet. For now we'll do nothing to disturb them and hope the wolves will make it."

"They will, Julia," Pilar assured her. "It is as it should be, with the animals in the desert where they belong. It is God's will."

Julia smiled her thanks. Pilar and her husband, Luis, had supported the project from the beginning, convinced that Julia, Rafe and their team from the university were restoring the order that was meant to be.

"I wish everyone felt the way you do," she said fervently.

"They will in time," Pilar told her. "Now what can I get for you today?"

"Actually, I don't need anything. I just stopped in for a visit."

"You won't leave empty-handed," Pilar insisted. "We have fresh-baked bread for tonight and pastry for tomorrow." She wrapped two loaves of bread and a dozen pastries in brown paper and tucked them into a bag, which she gave to Julia, waving off her offer to pay. "This is a gift. For bringing Rafael home to us and for bringing back the wolves."

"Pilar, please, you give me too much."

Julia's argument fell upon deaf ears. It was impossible to avoid Pilar's generosity. Even when she managed to pay for her groceries, Pilar always slipped a little something special into one of the bags.

Julia waved goodbye and continued her walk, thinking about Rafe's family. How lucky she was to have his parents' affection spill over onto her!

She crossed the road near the end of Main Street. Her destination was the sheriff's office in a small corner building. Jake was the real reason she'd come to town. After her conversation with Rafe, Julia had realized that she'd have to talk to the sheriff to let *him* know *she* knew what he was up to.

As she approached his office, Julia's heart pounded a few beats faster. There was absolutely no reason for that to happen, she lectured herself. This wasn't even a social call, really. At least, she didn't mean it to be one.

She walked into the empty reception room and thought for a moment he'd left. Then she heard his voice and followed the sound down a hallway.

"Yeah, Joe. We can do that for you. Sure, it's no problem."

He was facing the door and watched her walk into the office. He shifted the telephone to his other shoulder, a surprised look on his face.

"I'll discuss that with you later, Joe. Something's come up." He got rid of the caller and put down the phone. Then after a long beat of silence he smiled and stood up. "Well, Dr. Shelton. What a surprise. Here to report a crime?"

"Sort of," she replied vaguely as she took in his office. It was unusually well organized. File folders were stacked neatly on the desk; in the Out box were a few signed letters with envelopes attached; the In box was empty. It looked like the office of a man who was obsessively neat, or a man whose heart wasn't really in his job.

"In that case, please sit down," he offered, "and fill out an official report for me."

"I think this should be more . . . unofficial," she told him.

"That intrigues me, Julia." He used her first name easily.

That irritated her. He was so at ease that she felt just the opposite. She was trying to be serious, and he was teasing.

He was flirting with her, and that was exactly what she wanted to avoid. She took a deep breath and plunged in. "I know what you're up to, Sheriff, and I know why. Actually, you're the guilty party in this."

His gaze never wavered, and his eyes never lost their playful look. "So, I'm found out at last. Well, I expect that I'm guilty of many things. Which one is it you've caught me at?"

She ignored the teasing and went on. "Your connection with Fred Gilmer."

Jake raised an eyebrow.

"I know that you're his right-hand man. In fact, I know you two are thick as thieves."

"Bad comparison," he observed.

She ignored him again. "I also know that he's the one who wants me watched and that he's just waiting for me to make a mistake, commit some misdemeanor or violate some obscure law. It's not going to happen, though, and you can tell Mr. Gilmer exactly that."

Now she definitely had his attention. His green eyes had narrowed fractionally, and when he spoke, his voice had just the hint of an edge. "Just how did you get your information?"

"I have my sources," she said, rather proud of herself.

"Well, they're wrong. I'm not Fred Gilmer's man. I belong to no one. I'm the sheriff of this whole county, and it's my job to look out for all its citizens. I've told you that before, but obviously you don't choose to believe me."

"Let's put our cards on the table, Sheriff."

"Gladly, Dr. Shelton."

She leaned toward his desk. "You're watching me, so I'm going to return the compliment. I'm going to watch you watching me, so I'll have some kind of control over the information you feed Fred Gilmer."

Jake sat back in his chair, hands locked behind his head. She was the damnedest woman he'd ever met. She flew a line as direct as a homing pigeon. And she'd made that comment about being in control. He'd store it away for the future. It might come in handy somewhere down the line.

"Well, all this sounds pretty interesting to me. I can't think of anyone I'd rather watch, or be watched by. How exactly does this work? Do we move in together?" He raised a questioning eyebrow.

"I'm neither teasing nor propositioning you," Julia retorted. "I'm deadly serious about this. And for your information, here's how it works: you learn about the project, see the good in it, and report to Gilmer that not only are we law-abiding, we're enriching everyone's life around here."

"Especially mine," he murmured, "but it sounds okay to me. I like your plan just fine. I'll certainly learn all I can about the project, remembering to look for the good in it. Now, how do we start?"

"Actually, my car's in the shop, so we could start with you giving me a ride home."

She hadn't planned that, at least not consciously. Yet she'd refused Rafe's and the mechanic's offers of rides. Having voiced the suggestion, Julia regretted it and retracted quickly.

"It's all right," she said. "You have work to do, and the mechanic can easily drive me home."

But it was too late.

"Oh, no," Jake said. "You're not getting out of that. The offer's made. I accept."

"But you're working...."

Jake laughed. "You can see how busy I am. I have a part-time secretary who's *very* part-time. When we're both out, phone calls are picked up at the fire station, and I wear a beeper. I'll just switch the phone over now." He picked up the receiver and dialed.

Julia had no further excuses.

"Ready?" he asked, hanging up.

Julia glanced at her watch. "Yes, it's time for me to get the computer booted up. You might find that interesting."

Jake frowned and reached for his hat. Staring at a computer screen wasn't his idea of fun, but staring at it with Julia beside him was more than acceptable. Besides, they couldn't spend *all* day bent over blinking lights, could they?

"THERE'RE USUALLY six to eight wolves in a pack," Julia told him as she called up the program on the computer.

"Always an Alpha male and female, the leaders of the pack. See their blips—right there!" She pointed them out excitedly. "Alpha One and Alpha Two."

"Which is the boy and which is the girl?" Jake asked with a smile.

Julia was happy to respond. "The female is Alpha One. She's a fine wolf, strong and smart—and loyal."

"I'm not surprised," Jake said. He watched the blips and tried to remember what he'd read about tracking animals in the wild so he could come up with an intelligent question. "Are they wearing collars?"

He remembered her mentioning something about the tracking on their first visit, but he'd been as uninterested in the wolves then as he was now. Even if he had cared about the answer, he was sure he wouldn't be able to concentrate on it, not with Julia's scent swirling around him. It was faint but pervasive, less strong than perfume. It could be shampoo, he decided. She didn't seem the kind of woman who'd buy herself fancy perfumes. He hadn't seen any in her room, either.

The realization hit Jake hard. He suddenly wanted to indulge her, shower her with perfume, flowers, gifts, and became aware that he was getting a little carried away, just thinking about the possibilities. She brought out a multitude of feelings in him, some obvious, some still below the surface and unidentifiable.

But Julia clearly wasn't going to give him a chance to romanticize. She nodded. "They're radio transmitters, which give off signals that we pick up and transfer to the blips on the computer. I can tell the difference between the Alpha and Beta wolves by the sound," she told him.

"That's, uh . . ."

"I know, not too exciting," Julia answered with a smile of her own.

"No, it's intriguing. What about the other wolves? Can you identify them, too?"

Julia knew he was teasing her, but she was determined to be serious. "There're six in all. Two younger males and two females." In fact, she couldn't identify them yet, so she avoided the question with more information. "Only the Alphas will breed. Alpha One is pregnant now and she'll give birth in the summer if nothing goes wrong."

"I'm sure nothing will," he said encouragingly, and Julia couldn't detect any sign of sarcasm.

"I hope you're right," she said. Once again, she began to laugh. "I sound like a doting mother. Which I am," she admitted, turning to look up at Jake.

The sparkle in her eyes was for *wolves*, he reminded himself, willing his hands to stay by his sides. He was very close to putting them around her waist or leaning forward, just a little closer, so that his lips could touch her cheek.

She turned back to the screen and said, "They're moving out a little from the original territory. That's good. As it gets darker, they probably will wander farther, exploring."

"What happens when the young ones are born?" he asked, still trying to feign interest.

"They'll be all right because the whole pack will help take care of the pups. That's what's special about wolves. They're family oriented, very social animals." Her attention was still focused on the screen. "Now they seem to have stopped. Something probably spooked them."

For a while Jake watched with her, then began to tire. Finally he said, "I hate to suggest this, but isn't it possible to record the tracking, so you don't have to hang over the screen and watch all day?"

Julia chuckled. "Not only possible, but instantly obtainable." She hit two keys simultaneously and turned from the monitor. "You'll have to be patient with me. Today was our first day in the wild."

"You mean the wolves' first day in the wild, don't you?"

"I guess I *am* getting a little carried away." She glanced at him. "But I wanted you to see what happens. Tomorrow Rafe and I will analyze the recorded tracking data, and we'll be able to follow their movements and even learn whether they've made a kill or need to be fed. We'll plot them on the big map on the wall over there and maybe take the truck and do a little land tracking. It's all under control. I just wanted you to tell that to Gilmer."

"I don't have to tell him, Julia. I see what you're doing here, and I'm impressed by the professionalism."

"Thank you," she said.

"But even pros have to have a break now and then. Why don't you let me take you to dinner?" he ventured.

Julia shook her head. "I'm sorry, but I can't, Jake. Even though I'm recording, I need to be here to monitor the screen occasionally in case something goes wrong. It's too soon for me to be taking time off."

"What about when you took your car to town?" he asked, hoping to find a hole in her excuse.

"They weren't active that early," she answered.

Jake shrugged, wondering if he'd ever have a chance to take this dedicated and determined woman to dinner. "You have to eat." He was being insistent, which was not his usual style, but style had nothing to do with what he was feeling at the moment.

"True. But I can eat here," she said. "I've almost bought out the Santana store. Why don't you stay and have dinner with me?"

Julia hadn't meant to extend an invitation; it just happened. And it suddenly seemed quite appropriate.

"I'd like that," he said, adding, "I'm a pretty good cook."

"Great. You can be chef."

"I said 'pretty good,' Julia."

She laughed again as they got up and headed for the kitchen. "Okay, you can help me."

"That's more like it."

Julia began to pull ingredients for a salad out of the refrigerator, handing them to him. "Lettuce, peppers, mushrooms, carrots. That should be enough," she said. "Can you chop?"

"Like a master." Jake began to shred the lettuce into a big wooden bowl that stood ready.

"How about a beer while you work?"

"A soft drink will be fine," he answered.

She opened the refrigerator again and handed him a can of cola. "Still on duty?"

Jake hesitated a moment before answering. He knew his eyes were measuring her, and she must have felt it. After a moment she looked up at him questioningly. He decided to tell her. After all, he thought, she was nothing if not direct; he might as well follow suit. It was better for her to know now than later, better for him, too, because he'd be able to read her reaction. He'd gotten used to doing that.

"I never drink, Julia," he said. "I'm a recovering alcoholic." He watched her face closely and waited for her response.

"Oh," she said finally. "I feel so foolish."

That wasn't at all the response he expected. "Why?" he asked. "You didn't know. You couldn't have known. Unless, of course, your secret source was privy to the information. Obviously that wasn't the case."

"Obviously," she repeated. "Well, it doesn't really matter, does it?"

"It matters to me, but it shouldn't to anyone else. By the way, if you want beer or wine, please have it. I'm not the arbitrator of anyone else's life."

"Nope. I need to keep a clear head for my work tonight." After a pause she made another unexpected observation. "I suppose Fred Gilmer knows about your alcoholism?"

"You get right to the point, don't you?"

"I guess so. Are you chopping?"

"I'm chopping," Jake said, quickly picking up the knife. "Yes, Fred knows about my drinking problem. In fact, he knows just about everything there is to know about me. We go way back, and he's not such a bad guy, Julia. When you meet him, you'll realize that."

"Mmm." The sound was noncommittal; Julia returned to the refrigerator and took out a box of eggs. "I think I'll make an omelet while you chop."

"Good idea. " Julia clearly wasn't ready to believe what he said about Fred. He glanced at her, but she only smiled.

"Chop," she told him, so he did.

They stood side by side working at the counter, and Jake felt a kind of peace, an understanding between them that he hadn't felt with anyone for a very long while.

By the time Julia had checked her monitor one more time and they'd sat down for dinner, he knew he was going to tell her more. He might not reveal everything, but he'd tell her some. There was something about her that made him want to be as honest with Julia as she was with him.

"The omelet's great," he said.

"You're an easy man to please. The salad's good, too."

"You're an easy woman to please."

They smiled at each other and then without further hesitation he said, "Fred and I were in Vietnam together. Did you know about that?"

She nodded.

It was almost easy to go on. "After Vietnam I drifted for a while from job to job, place to place. Finally ended up in L.A. and got hired on at a detective agency. A big one. Very successful."

"Sounds exciting," she observed, "all those fast cars and shiny guns and beautiful women."

He nodded. "Yes, there was all of that. Pretty heady stuff."

"Who were your clients?"

"Hollywood types who wanted us to spy on their wives, studio heads who were checking up on their actors, movie stars who wanted to know what their girlfriends—and boyfriends—were up to."

"And you became a part of that jaded life-style?"

"Yes. It was catching. Big expense accounts, the best hotels, lots of bars and parties where the booze flowed much too freely. After a while I just couldn't keep up with it anymore. Couldn't deal with it, I guess."

"Vietnam must have had something to do with that," Julia commented.

"Maybe, but I'm not making any excuses. I went downhill fast, really hit the skids, lost my job, got into debt and into big trouble. Fred heard about it and offered me a job out here—if I got cleaned up. So I did."

"He gave you the sheriff's job? I thought that was elective."

"It is. Fred gave me a job working for him, I ran for sheriff the following year—and got elected on my own." He smiled at her. "But Fred came to my rescue initially."

"That's why you're so loyal."

Jake looked at her across the table. "I wonder why it's a plus when it comes to the wolves, and yet you make it sound like something detrimental to human beings?"

Julia seemed startled by his observation. "I didn't mean that. I guess I was just adding up all the facts that went into your friendship with Fred Gilmer. That's what we scientists do. It's not very personal."

"No," he agreed, "but it's very sensible, and you are definitely the sensible type."

Jake wasn't sure just how she took that, but it was okay, because he wasn't sure just how he meant it, either. This whole conversation was getting a little confusing, and he wanted to get away from the emphasis on Fred and himself. He wanted to talk about her.

Yet somehow he just couldn't find the right way to turn the conversation, and that really confused him. He had never had any trouble finding out everything about the women who'd come into his life; usually something about him seemed to make them reveal every intimate detail. Not so Julia.

"Now that you know about my deep, dark secrets, Madame Scientist, what about yours?"

"After coffee," she promised.

3

THEY WALKED across the desert, not touching, but close enough for Julia to be very aware of Jake, a tall and imposing figure beside her, shortening his long strides to match hers.

The moon played hide-and-seek behind the clouds and silhouetted the twisted shapes of cacti against the sky. Julia's thoughts ricocheted from her wolves to Jake Forrester. He was too close, too much of a presence in the heavy night air for her to ignore. An intriguing man, he was more complex than she'd first perceived.

He broke the silence. "Okay, it's your turn now."

Julia's gaze was quizzical. "My turn for what?"

"You promised to share your secrets after we finished our coffee. Well, we're all done, Julia. So let's hear 'em."

"I only have one secret," she said.

"I'm all ears, lady."

"Simple. My secret is that I have no secrets. I'm just an average kind of woman, living an average kind of life."

"Sure, sure," Jake agreed. "Most women I know raise wolves out in the middle of nowhere."

"Better four-legged wolves than the two-legged kind, my granny always used to tell me," she bantered.

He looked down at her, smiling. Her teasing didn't faze him. "I don't know much about the four-legged kind, but I'd be more than willing to hear all about the ones with two legs," he drawled, "and how they fit into your life."

When she didn't reply, he continued unabashed. "All right. Let's put it in plain words. Are there any men in your life, Julia?"

"Not at this moment," she said, looking him squarely in the eye, and trying to ignore the romantic impulses provoked by the sight of Jake in the moonlight.

"You're making it tough. I thought you were Miss Tell-it-like-it-is."

"I'm just teasing, Sheriff," she admitted.

"Why?" he asked, pressing her for an honest reply.

Julia started walking back toward the house. Jake followed at a leisurely pace, giving her a few moments to gather her thoughts before he caught up with her.

"When I said there wasn't much to tell, I meant it," she finally said.

"Not much. But something?"

"Yes. I was seeing someone at the university." She paused, not used to exposing herself and unsure why she was tempted to do so now.

"Go on," he insisted, and for some reason she opened up to Jake Forrester, a man she hardly knew.

"I guess you'd call it a 'long-term relationship.' Isn't that the catchphrase these days?" Not waiting for Jake's reply, she went on. "Ted and I weren't in the same department at the university, but his work and mine often brought us together."

"Maybe he was into computers?" Jake speculated.

"Smart guess," she said. "Most of the university was 'into computers' in some kind of way, but Ted was in the behavioral sciences department. He studied and observed human and animal behavior patterns, and that was where I came in."

"So?"

"So we had similar interests, we were both workaholics, dedicated and all that. Our friends in the faculty thought we were destined to be together."

"Then why didn't it work out with you and Mr. Dedication?"

"Maybe because we were too much alike, so wound up in our work that it overshadowed the rest of life. Ted had his studies, I had mine. Then—" Julia hesitated.

"Then?" Jake prompted.

"Then Ted got a chance to work on a project overseas...."

"And you each went your own way."

Their steps slowed as they reached the house. "Yes," she said. "I don't believe that either of us gave a moment's thought to my going with him. We talked about getting together, meeting somewhere glamorous like the Riviera, but we never seemed to have time for it to happen. I guess that also says something about us."

"Or about him," Jake suggested. "Maybe he didn't have what it takes to keep a woman like you interested."

She was standing on the step above him. In the bright moonlight they could see each other clearly. "And what would it take to keep me interested, Sheriff? I'm sure you have an idea."

He laughed, a low, sexy sound that sent chills running along Julia's spine. She tried to ignore them, but it was impossible. Besides, her heart was beating to a crazy rhythm that his soft laughter had triggered.

"I have lots of ideas about you, lady. Lots and lots of ideas."

Jake moved toward her slightly, and Julia meant to move away, but for some reason she stayed just where she was, looking at him in the moonlight, waiting, knowing he was going to kiss her.

He didn't. Instead he reached up and touched her face with his fingertips. She smiled at him and turned away. She climbed the last step to the porch.

He caught her hand in his, pulling her gently to him, so gently that she wasn't able to resist. His lips brushed hers and his arms encircled her, holding her close. The fabric of his shirt rubbed against her tender nipples, adding more sensations to those already cascading through her.

Julia knew she had to get away from him now or it would be too late. The lips that had touched hers so softly were now on her cheek, her neck. His breath was warm, and her own caught in her throat, preventing her from speaking.

Finally she found her voice. "Jake, uh, Sheriff . . ."

"Yes, Dr. Shelton?"

"I—" She was speechless again. He'd moved his lips to her ear.

"You're not interested in continuing our research?" he asked teasingly.

"No, I'm not," she managed. His tongue had just slipped into her ear, languidly probing its sensitive shell. Instead of pushing away, as she'd meant to do, Julia found herself leaning against him. She could feel the long, hard muscles of his thighs against her. Then his mouth was on hers again, not fleetingly, not hesitantly, but hot and demanding.

If she'd only moved away sooner... But she hadn't, and now it was too late for Julia to resist. She opened her lips under his and returned the kiss eagerly. His tongue claimed hers, probing the recesses of her mouth, getting to know her thoroughly.

Julia gave herself up to the magic, to the headiness of the kiss, then uttered a little moan and forced herself to step away, running her fingers across her lips. As if to remember what had happened between them—or to wipe it away?

Confused, she couldn't be sure what the gesture had meant. She only knew that she could feel the heat of her cheeks and a wild, uncontrollable trembling inside. Jake must have seen her flushed face, sensed the trembling, because he reached for her again.

Struggling to gain control over her racing emotions, Julia stepped away a second time. She saw him smile, as if they shared some kind of secret. He climbed the steps, stood beside her and put one hand upon her shoulder, his thumb resting on the rise of her breast. Julia knew he could feel the wild thumping of her heart and willed it to slow down.

He stroked her shoulder as he spoke. "You're delectable, Dr. Shelton. I think it's time for some on-the-spot research."

The arrogance of his tone alerted Julia. "You're very sure of yourself, aren't you?" she inquired, hearing the strain, the huskiness in her voice, a voice far less strong than her words.

"What's wrong with the idea of research?" he asked teasingly.

"It's fine—in its place."

"And maybe the porch isn't the place. Inside, then?"

Julia shook her head, not willing to trust her voice this time.

"Let's just go for the moment, Julia," he suggested.

"No," she said decisively. "It's not the time or the place, Sheriff." Regaining some of her composure, Julia removed his hand from her shoulder.

"Don't tell me you're afraid of the big, bad wolf?" Her refusal didn't seem to faze him; he was still laughing.

"Of course I'm not." She was beginning to feel defensive now, aware that she hadn't quite won the battle against his overt sensuality. "I need to keep a clear head out here in the desert. My work is important, and I'm certainly not going to bed with the opposition."

"Who said anything about bed?" he asked innocently.

"I ..." She groped unsuccessfully for a quick answer.

"There's a nice sofa in the den. There's a great big kitchen table. . . ."

"You are impossible, Jake Forrester, and we are definitely calling this a night."

He gave a little shrug. "Whatever you say, Doc. But there will be other moonlit nights and we'll share one of them soon. I'll guarantee it."

He stood there towering above her, solid, self-assured and grinning. Julia couldn't control the urge to take him down a peg. "But can you guarantee that this isn't some Fred Gilmer plan to get me sidetracked?"

The remark seemed to serve only to amuse him. "Honey, tonight was all my idea. Well," he amended, "that's not altogether true."

"You see, I knew your pal Gilmer—"

"I didn't mean Gilmer. I meant you."

"What?" This wasn't going the way she'd hoped.

"That's right, Julia. Tonight was my idea—and yours, if you'd only admit it." With that he bent to drop a light kiss upon her lips. Then he was gone.

JULIA SANG ALOUD as she made the morning coffee. It was because of the wolves, she told herself. They were adjusting marvelously, and so far the project was on the road to success. Her need to break into song had nothing to do with last night or Jake Forrester. Nothing at all.

•

When she heard a vehicle outside, Julia knew immediately it didn't belong to Rafe or Jake. It was amazing how living out in the middle of nowhere seemed to sharpen all her senses. She went to the door in time to see a young woman climb out of a low-slung blue sports car and approach the cabin, her blond hair shining in the early-morning sun. It was the car that held Julia's attention; it didn't seem to fit in Pierson County, where Jeeps and pickup trucks were the transportation of choice.

The woman bounded up the steps in an appealing youthful, carefree manner.

"Hi, I'm Beth. Beth Gilmer," she said in a soft, lilting voice, crossing the porch toward Julia, hand extended.

Julia's secret sigh was almost audible. There it was again, the Gilmer name. Somehow she'd known the feelings she awakened with were too good to last. "Fred Gilmer's daughter?" she asked, taking the proffered hand.

"Guilty," Beth responded.

"I'm Julia Shelton."

"Of course, I know that. I know all about you."

"Then come on in and have some coffee."

Still mystified by the visit and sure this latest Gilmer connection was bound to be trouble, Julia gave Beth the obligatory tour of the house and waited to find out what the unscheduled visit was all about over coffee.

Beth talked animatedly about the house, which, she claimed, had intrigued her since childhood. While she chatted away, Julia had a chance to observe the young woman. Beth *was* young, in her early twenties, and definitely very pretty, with fair skin, blue eyes and a slim, athletic body. In one word, Beth Gilmer was classy, Julia thought. She wore top-of-the-line sneakers, linen walking shorts and a creamy silk shirt, her ensemble a far cry from Julia's cutoff jeans and T-shirt.

At last, her coffee finished, Beth flashed a smile that would have made the lights of Las Vegas seem dim. "I guess you wonder why I'm here."

Julia smiled. "The question did enter my mind."

"Well, I've come to volunteer." Beth made the pronouncement as if she were bestowing a gift upon Julia.

Volunteer? Fred Gilmer, head of the Cattlemen's Association, had a daughter who wanted to volunteer for the wolf project? Something was very wrong here. Julia wondered if Gilmer was sending two spies against her, first Jake and now Beth. Well, she had to respond, and now wasn't the time for subtlety.

"But your father—"

Beth dismissed him with a wave of her hand. "Oh, Daddy. He doesn't understand anything about what you're doing, Julia. I can call you Julia, can't I? He has these prehistoric ideas that wolves roam in packs and kill herds of cattle and steal little babies they eat for dinner."

"Well, they do roam in packs," Julia confirmed.

"Any reading on the subject will prove that wolves are hardly a threat to cattle these days."

"You've been reading up on wolves?" Julia asked.

Beth paused momentarily. "Just a few articles here and there. When I found out you were in Pierson County, I spent an afternoon at the library. I discovered some really interesting studies. If everyone would read them, you wouldn't have any problem. Unfortunately," she added with a shake of her head, "that's not going to happen, so my suggestion is that you get the word out locally." She beamed another brilliant smile.

"Well, that's very interesting, Beth, but—"

"Seriously, you have to win over the community if this project is going to work."

She had a point, Julia admitted. Even the university had suggested she get to know the people of Pierson County, but that aspect of the job was something Julia usually avoided.

"I'd planned to leave that to my assistant," she said, "but he's been so busy with the fieldwork, there just hasn't been time. As for myself, I'm not a people person." She frowned slightly, hating the catchphrase. "I'm no good at making contacts, and I'm even worse at making speeches."

Beth sat back, a pleased look on her face. "And that's why I'm here, Julia," she announced.

Julia started to object, but Beth was clearly determined to make her point. "I'm great with people. I've just graduated from college with a degree in public relations. Where better to put it to use than here in your wolf project? This is perfect!" she declared.

"Now, wait, whoa!" Julia exclaimed, managing to squeeze in her objections. "Slow down a minute."

Somehow she had to put the skids on Beth and her youthful enthusiasm. There was more than one objection to having Beth work on the project, so she began with the most obvious one.

"The truth is, Beth, your father doesn't like my being here, and your working with us could make the situation very unpleasant. I'm sure that's something we'd all like to avoid."

Beth remained calm. "I'd be very surprised if you declined to take me on, just because of what my father is or thinks or might do. I want to be judged by who *I* am and what *I* can accomplish, not who my father is. You're a professional, Dr. Shelton. I'm sure you can understand that."

Julia realized then that not only was Beth Gilmer pretty and enthusiastic, she was also intelligent and tough-minded. Her response had been perfect, right down to the not-so-subtle use of Julia's title. One professional woman to another. She had to smile. "I can't argue with you about that, Beth. If you have good ideas about the project, I'd like to hear them and judge for myself. However, I can't put my work in jeopardy by hiring—so to speak—the daughter of someone who is clearly against our success. I'm sure *you* can understand that."

"I can and do," Beth responded. "Whatever my father's opinions, they won't be any more adamant if I come to work here. I doubt if they'll be any less adamant, either, to tell you the truth. But I can guarantee not to do anything detrimental to the project."

"Fine," Julia said, accepting her assurance. "That's all I needed to hear. Now tell me how you can be a help."

"That's easy," Beth said. "First I'd place a few articles in the area newspapers. I'm surprised you haven't had some requests already."

Julia thought guiltily about the unanswered letters and phone calls from the media tucked beneath the blotter on her desk.

"Then," Beth continued, "I'd try to change the attitude of the community, and the best place to do that is through the grass roots. Get in touch with the schools, the churches, the local organizations. In fact, I have a fabulous idea." She charged ahead.

"You know, of course, about the success of the whale project out of New England. Certain free-swimming whales were adopted by groups and individuals all over the United States. The adoptive parents, if you could call them that, get photos and information on the whale's migration. What it does is personalize the animals, and if a whale—or a wolf—belongs to someone, then it's going to be safer and more protected. People will start to care."

"So you want local groups—children—to adopt my wolves?"

"It's an incredible idea, Julia, even if I did come up with it myself—sort of."

Julia had to admit that it was a good idea, but she could see pitfalls as well as possibilities. It would mean an entirely new direction for the project, certainly unscientific but perhaps productive. She was mulling it over when she heard the sound of the truck, followed by Rafe's footsteps on the porch.

Rafe had obviously recognized the sports car. His face showed a mixture of emotions—welcome, wariness, excitement, regret.

Beth, on the other hand, was all pleasure. "Rafe, what a wonderful surprise!"

Julia doubted if Beth was surprised at all, but gave Rafe the facts. "Beth has volunteered to help out on the project since we're short of funds and long on work."

She waited for Rafe's response. If he showed any reluctance, Julia would politely but firmly say no to Beth's offer.

"What a great idea," he observed, his words not entirely matching the look in his eyes. "We need all the help we can get. Are you back in Pierson County for good, Beth?" Rafe made no move to leave his position in the doorway.

"I'm not sure. Maybe."

"Beth would like to organize community support for us by contacting local groups and trying to get them to understand what we're doing."

"That's a great idea," Rafe repeated, his attention still focused on Beth. "So you may be around for a while, at least?"

"As long as it takes, assuming Julia decides to take me on."

"I just decided to," Julia said, holding out her hand. "Welcome aboard."

Beth shook it enthusiastically, then focused again on Rafe. "I'd like to start a Save Our Wolves Project," she told him. "Maybe—do you think—would your mom like to help?"

"She'd love to," Rafe answered.

"She knows everyone in town," Beth told Julia.

"That's true," he agreed. "She was at school often enough when all us kids were growing up, so she knows all the teachers. Some of them may even have forgotten the trouble my brothers and I managed to cause. My sisters were usually getting awards of some kind or another. Plus Mom's at church whenever the doors open."

"She'll be a fantastic help," Beth said.

"And she's already enthusiastic about the project."

"That's great," Julia put in, but the two young people were still staring at each other and paying very little attention to her.

"I'd like to see your mother," Beth said. "It's been years."

"Years . . ." Rafe echoed.

Julia decided to interrupt before the two of them ended up in each other's arms. She cleared her throat. "So," she said brightly, "we're all agreed. Beth will be working on community relations on a volunteer basis, which will leave Rafe and me to concentrate on the project—a full-time job," she added for Beth's benefit. "Since our time for PR will be limited, Beth, you'll have to carry most of the load. We'll meet periodically to discuss details. You'll need to keep a list of all your contacts, give me some kind of written report."

Beth and Rafe were still sharing an intimate gaze that seemed to Julia as sensual as if they'd been locked in each other's arms.

"So," she said, picking up a stack of files, "I guess our first staff meeting is officially adjourned."

Beth finally looked at Julia. "Right. I think I'll start by dropping by the store and visiting Mrs. Santana. Might as well get into the work right away. Oh, I'll need information on all the wolves—photos, if you have them, names and ages."

Rafe came to life before Julia could reply. "I can do that for you. Then maybe we can work out a time to get together." He turned to Julia. "I'll walk Beth to her car. It'll just take a minute, and then we can get to the wolves."

Beth took Julia's hand. "I'll do a good job, I promise. Thanks for giving me the chance." At the door she paused. "I almost forgot. We're having our annual barbecue Saturday night at the house, and you're both invited. With your dates," she added, looking at Rafe.

"That's very nice, Beth," Julia said, "but are you sure your father won't object—?"

"It's my party, too," Beth interrupted. "Daddy loves to add new people. Please come." The invitation clearly included Rafe.

"I'll certainly try," was all Julia would promise.

It wasn't enough for Beth. "It's going to be the event of the year," she said without conceit. "Everyone in Pierson County will be there—lots of people you should meet because they can help with the project."

"Then how can I refuse?" Julia asked rhetorically, knowing it was already a fait accompli. Apparently, Beth Gilmer always got what she wanted.

"See you Saturday, then." Rafe held the door open for Beth.

Julia peeked out the window and watched them talking beside the little car. Whatever the feelings had been between Rafe and Beth, it was obvious that the attraction was still strong—even to someone as unromantic and pragmatic as Julia.

"Trouble," she muttered, stepping away from the window. "It can't be anything but trouble."

Rafe and Beth. Gilmer and Jake. Julia would have to keep them all in balance to ensure the success of her project. While Beth's motives were clearly suspect, her ideas were interesting, even exciting. She'd be a hard worker, and Rafe had already proved himself. There was, however, no way to predict what would happen with Jake, and as for Fred Gilmer, the party would give Julia the opportunity to size him up. She was looking forward to it.

THE PHONE RANG at nearly eleven o'clock that night, when Julia was reading computer printouts. She answered it absently.

"Wake you up, Doc?"

The sound of Jake's voice surprised her. "No," she said, "I was burning the midnight oil, which probably accounts for my vagueness."

"Maybe you need a little company to bring you back to reality."

"This *is* reality," she assured him. "And I don't need any company."

"Sure?" he persisted.

"Positive. I told you, I'm quite happy out here alone."

"Mmm," he said, sounding unconvinced. "I'll bet even the dedicated Dr. Shelton needs a little R and R sometimes. How about going with me to the Gilmers' party on Saturday night?"

"I'd love to," Julia answered without a moment's hesitation, only to be greeted by complete silence at the other end of the line. "Jake? Are you there?"

He chuckled. "Yep. Just stunned. I didn't even have a chance to argue or tell you about the event."

"I already know about it."

"Oh? How's that?"

"Word gets around," Julia replied, not inclined to go into the afternoon's occurrences.

"And I thought I was going to have to beg and wheedle," he said, not pressing her for an explanation.

"Sometimes I can be cooperative." Jake was bound to take her comment and come up with a suggestive response. Quickly she added, "What better way to walk into the lion's den than on the arm of another lion?"

She heard another chuckle. "Then put your dancing shoes on, Julia, honey. I'll see you Saturday night around seven."

Dancing shoes? Julia hung up, went into her room and opened the closet door. There were no dancing shoes among her boots and sneakers. She flipped through her clothes. A few dresses, suitable for faculty teas and press conferences, but nothing special, nothing exciting. None of them would do.

It had been a long time since Julia had wanted a fantastic dress. It was time to pay a visit to a shopping mall.

"I need to make a good impression," she said to herself, "so the good citizens of Pierson County will realize that I'm a force to be reckoned with."

She didn't voice the thought that followed. *And wouldn't it be nice if Jake Forrester was knocked right off his feet?*

4

"WELL, WELL. Little Red Riding Hood. You look good enough to eat."

Julia blushed, embarrassed and pleased by Jake's outburst of admiration. She walked down the porch steps to meet him.

"You look pretty good yourself, Sheriff." He was out of uniform, handsome in a light blue shirt and pale gray slacks. He wore no tie, and she knew she was right on target about the dress for the Gilmer barbecue: women in fancy clothes, men in casual.

Jake circled around her and let out a low whistle. "That's quite a dress, Julia. And I'd always heard redheads couldn't wear that color."

He was right. Most redheads didn't look good in flame red, but Julia had always been an exception. She'd decided to spend a small fortune on the sundress with its inset lace panels, and never had any doubt about the color.

"I'm glad you like it," she said, a little flustered by his intensive scrutiny. "I decided to make a good impression tonight."

"Oh, you will, you definitely will," Jake assured her; he took her hand and led her to the Jeep. "I can't wait to show you off."

She hadn't anticipated that he'd grab her around the waist and lift her onto the seat. She'd never been helped into a car—of any kind—quite like that, and she smiled, amused. Jake was a two-legged wolf, no doubt about it, but as long as she kept that in mind, Julia planned to enjoy herself in his company.

It was her turn to be impressed when they drove down the road toward the Gilmer ranch house. The brick walls glowed in the setting sun. Two stories high, it was faced with a wraparound porch and innumerable white columns, more suited to the antebellum South than to the desert.

They were met by a horde of valets, and when they climbed the wide steps onto the porch, a liveried doorman ushered them inside. Rugs covered the terra-cotta-tiled floor, a huge staircase curved upward toward the second floor, and expensive, lavish furnishings added to the air of luxury.

"Your friend has good taste," she observed.

"This was all his wife's doing," Jake told her. "Lucy's ancestral ties were to the Old South, and she was determined that this place should reflect her background. Unfortunately, she died when Beth was a teenager."

"That's very sad," Julia murmured.

"Yes, it is, but Lucy had a chance to enjoy the house for many years. Now come on. The real party is happening outside."

The central focus of the backyard was a huge, kidney-shaped pool. It was ringed by long tables laden with food. On one side stood an expansive bar. A huge side of beef was rotating on the barbecue spit, permeating the air with the smell of roasting meat. Masses of red and white flowers bloomed profusely in clay pots, and colorful glowing lanterns cast a romantic glow over the gathering crowd.

The sun had barely set, but the party was already in full swing. Under the white canopy of a tent, a country-and-western band was going strong, and dozens of couples crowded the dance floor, cowboy boots and strappy high heels keeping time to the lively beat.

"What do you think?" Jake asked.

"I'd say this isn't a shy group of partygoers. As for the spread, the budget for all of it would support our project for a year," she whispered, breaking off as Beth appeared beside them.

"I'm so glad you came. You look gorgeous, Julia."

"Beth, you look stunning." She was wearing white, with her long, blond hair flowing around her shoulders; it gave her an ethereal quality.

"Come on," she urged, "I want you to meet Daddy."

"I'll get us some drinks," Jake volunteered. "What would you like, Julia?"

"White wine, please," Julia answered as Beth grabbed her hand and dragged her through the crowd.

Fred Gilmer immediately left the guests he was talking with when he caught sight of them. Julia could tell at once that he doted on the girl, and that knowledge failed to reassure her.

Julia thought about Lucy Gilmer, who had died at a time when Beth was a teenager. Fred had obviously carried out his parental duties with gusto, since he'd disapproved of Beth's friendship with Rafe.

"Daddy," Beth was saying, "this is Julia Shelton. You know, out at the Farrell ranch."

"Of course, *Dr.* Shelton. Good to meet you at last." He took her hand in a strong clasp. "I hear you're giving my little girl a chance to try out her skills."

"Yes, I was delighted that she volunteered," Julia said, making it clear that Beth's involvement wasn't her idea at all.

"It'll be interesting to see what goes on out there," Gilmer went on. "I wish you success, and hope this project turns out just as you want it to."

Julia searched Fred's eyes. Although he'd spoken with a jolly sort of sincerity, she wasn't deceived for a moment. She'd heard a challenge in his words. It had been subtle, but she knew that was his strategy.

"I hope it will, too." They looked at each other for a long moment. Julia didn't let her gaze wander. He was sizing her up, and she wasn't going to back down. Finally Fred smiled and looked away, but Julia still felt good. He knew now what he was up against.

"I want you and Jake to have a great time here tonight," he said, then quickly surveyed his domain. "We've got plenty to eat and plenty to drink and there'll be dancing all night. You do dance, don't you?"

"I certainly do," Julia replied.

"Good, I'll look for you later," he promised.

She felt a little shiver inside. She'd passed the inspection, but didn't relish dancing with Fred Gilmer.

"Now, where's Jake?" Fred wanted to know. "Oh, there he is, talking to one of his lady friends. I'll tell you, Julia, he's broken plenty of hearts hereabouts. You watch out, honey." He turned and made his way through the crowd.

"He's just joking about Jake's girlfriends," Beth said hastily. "Daddy's a big teaser."

"I can imagine," Julia answered dryly. There'd been malice in Fred Gilmer's words, a warning that she could trust Jake only so far. Well, she knew that and was determined not to be made a fool of in front of the entire county.

Julia glanced around and caught sight of Jake deep in conversation with an exceptionally beautiful brunette. The tall, shapely woman held on to his arm and leaned close as they conversed.

"Jake used to date her a couple of years ago," Beth informed Julia, "then he dropped her, and she married someone else. I hear she's terribly unhappy."

"Poor thing," Julia said noncommittally, determined not to be drawn into gossip about Jake. "I think I'll wander over to the food table. It looks scrumptious."

She stepped away, only to hear Beth call after her. "Do you know when Rafe will be coming?"

"He didn't mention anything to me," Julia said, praying that he wouldn't show up.

She was standing at the edge of a crowd a few minutes later, dipping a blue corn tortilla into a mound of guacamole, when Jake materialized at her side and handed her a glass of wine. "Where'd you disappear to?"

"I could ask you the same thing."

"I know lots of people here."

"All of them women?"

She'd meant it as a joke, but knew she'd sounded jealous, which was totally out of character for her. So she breathed a sigh of relief when Jake laughed.

"Do I detect a little jealousy there, Doc? I hope so," he added.

"Not at all," she replied quickly. "Just an observation."

"Then could it possibly mean you missed me?"

"Desperately," she joked, falling in with his light mood.

"Then let's dance, shall we?" Jake took her wineglass and plate and put them on the table. "I've been waiting to get you into my arms."

The band was playing something soft and sad, a country-and-western ballad about a woman who loved her man and lost him and would never love again. Jake cradled Julia in his arms, resisting her attempts to put some distance between them.

It was an impossible situation. Julia knew his reputation. Fred's warning had made things perfectly clear, and tonight Julia had seen for herself. Yet here she was, her breasts pressed against Jake, his large hand securely placed in the middle of her back. To top it all, he was a marvelous dancer.

"Have I told you how much I like that dress?" he asked, whispering into her ear.

She nodded, trying unsuccessfully to concentrate on the music and ignore what his body was doing to hers. There was a tingling deep inside her, a heady awareness. He slipped both hands around her waist, pulling her hips to his.

"Bet you can't be wearing a lot underneath," he murmured. "There's not much room."

Julia had to smile. She was indeed wearing very little under her dress.

"Maybe I can investigate later."

When she didn't reply, he let his lips graze her hairline and dropped soft kisses along her temples. That was almost too much. Julia felt a surge of desire. She wanted to return Jake's kisses, taste his lips against hers. Fortunately the music ended at that moment, and she forced herself to step away. "Let's go mingle," she said a bit breathlessly. "I haven't met anyone but Fred, and Beth said all the heavy hitters from Pierson County would be here tonight."

"I'd say she was right about that," Jake agreed. "And if you want to meet them, you shall. *Anything* your heart desires tonight is yours."

Julia took a deep breath. Jake's habit of throwing in his own double meaning was clearly something she was going to have to get used to.

SHE MET ALL THE GUESTS as the evening progressed. Their voices and smiles were friendly enough, but she sensed an underlying wariness. These were cattlemen for the most part, and all cattlemen thought alike when it came to wolves in their territory.

Julia did her best to remain cordial, accepting invitations for Beth to speak at the Rotary Club and the Women's Service League. Public speaking wasn't on her own agenda; besides, Beth already knew the enemy.

She was trying to explain that to Beth and Jake when Rafe walked in.

Beth had seemed totally wrapped up in the idea of speaking engagements, intent on convincing her new boss of her ability to dissuade any naysayers. She forgot everything when she saw Rafe and rushed across the yard to join him.

Julia saw Fred in the crowd at that moment and felt a chill run up and down her spine. He'd been able to conceal his feelings about her project, but when he saw Rafe, anger, even hate, showed clearly in his expression.

Julia reached for Jake's arm. "Something's going to happen," she said fearfully. "I wish Rafe hadn't shown up."

"It'll be okay, Julia. This is a party, not a showdown. You're trying to make a B-grade Western out of this."

"But I saw the look on Fred's face."

"Don't expect him to be friendly to the kid. He's a protective father, but he's not a tyrant. Come on, let's dance."

Jake was right, and she was probably overreacting. "Let's sit this one out," she suggested. Dancing with Jake was dangerous. It gave her all kinds of ideas, none of them suitable. She needed to be on guard against him. After all, she was supposed to be working with him for the sake of the project, not falling under his spell. Enough women had apparently done that, she told herself, and most of them seemed to be here at the barbecue, casting jealous, suspicious looks her way.

"Okay, we'll sit this one out, but only one. I fully intend to get back on the dance floor with you soon. Would you like another drink?"

"And some barbecued beef, please."

"A girl after my own heart, with an appetite to match." Jake headed for the table.

Julia sank onto a wrought-iron bench to watch the party. She caught sight of Rafe and Beth on the dance floor, oblivious to everything except each other.

She saw Fred nod to a couple of his ranch hands who were drinking beer at the edge of the dance floor. One of them cut in on Beth and Rafe, then two more hands hustled Rafe smoothly into the shadows beyond the pool house.

Julia jumped to her feet immediately, looking for Jake. He was weaving carefully through the crowd toward her, balancing two plates and a glass of wine.

"Not easy, but I accomplished it. Barbecue, tortillas—"

"Jake, something's going on," she whispered urgently.

He put the plates down and handed her the glass. "Yep. A party and a woman with a big appetite. Here." He reached for one of the plates. "Dive into this."

"Jake, listen to me. Two men just elbowed Rafe off the dance floor."

Jake was instantly alert. "Which way did they go?"

"Come on, I'll show you." They circled the pool house and headed quickly through the night-damp grass, closing in on three figures silhouetted in the moonlight. Julia recognised Rafe easily.

"Look, Santana, we don't like your kind hanging around here." Julia shivered at the threat in the cowboy's voice.

He was much taller and heavier than Rafe.

"I have a right to be here, just as much as you, and I plan to stay around."

"Brave, ain't he?" the other cowboy jeered.

"Maybe we better see just how brave," the first taunted, raising his clenched fist.

Julia knew what was coming, but Jake moved quickly to intercede. He deflected a crushing blow, throwing the man off balance.

"All right, fellows," Jake said, sidestepping as the huge man almost went down. "Enough is enough."

"Just having a little fun, Sheriff," the smaller of the two answered. "Santana and I are buddies, and we were remembering old times."

"Yeah," Jake said, "times when it was all right for local men to beat up Mexicans. Well, those times are past, so I suggest you boys go on down to the bunkhouse and cool off while Rafe returns to the party with us."

"I can take care of myself," Rafe interjected.

"Sure you can," the giant agreed. "So why don't you just let us be, Sheriff? Santana don't want you here any more than we do."

"Well, I'm here, no matter what anyone wants. So get going, boys."

"Now, Sheriff . . ."

"You heard me," Jake insisted, "or would you prefer the lockup downtown?" His tone was cold and deliberate.

"You can't—"

"Yes, I can."

The two men stepped away reluctantly, turned once and looked back at Jake, then disappeared into the darkness. The big man called quietly, threateningly, "Learn your place, Santana, and stay in it."

"I think you should make yourself scarce, too, Rafe," Jake advised. "There's no use looking for trouble."

"I wasn't looking for it," Rafe argued. "All I wanted was to dance with Beth. That's not a crime. I have rights."

"Sure you do," Jake said easily, "but let's not push things tonight. Cool down, and let the cowboys do the same."

"Is that what your buddy Fred Gilmer wants?" Rafe's voice was hard, angry.

"Rafe," Julia broke in.

"It's okay, Julia. We're all a little hot under the collar," Jake said calmly.

"Especially those goons of Gilmer's. They'll never cool down, and you know it," Rafe said.

"Maybe not, Rafe, but if you take things easy tonight, I'll talk to Fred and tell him to keep his boys in check."

"Sure you will." Rafe's tone was sarcastic now.

Julia was about to speak again, but Jake stopped her. "Come on, you two. Let's get back to the party."

"Sorry, Julia," Rafe mumbled as they made their way back. "I didn't mean for you to get involved in this."

"It's all right, Rafe," she said. "Let's just try to have a good time for the rest of the night."

It wasn't going to be easy. Jake piled another plate with food for Julia, then went looking for Fred. She sat down at the table and kept an eye on Rafe. It was all she could do; she had lost her appetite.

Rafe made his way straight to Beth, as Julia had expected, but instead of dancing, the two stood quietly at the edge of the dance floor, talking. Close by, couples swayed to the beat of country music, but the two young people were still, as if in their own world. Julia sensed something special between them.

She saw Beth's hand fly to her mouth. Rafe was obviously telling her about the incident. Beth looked around as if in search of her father. Rafe caught her arm then and gave her a little shake. Julia understood what fear Beth must be feeling for Rafe.

Julia was surprised to find herself still trembling from the confrontation. She'd always considered herself brave and forthright, but up to now, had never been faced with violence. Verbal fireworks, yes; there was plenty of that in faculty meetings. The thought of a physical battle made her very uneasy, especially when she remembered the size of the brute who'd come so close to beating Rafe up.

Julia pushed her plate away. It was time to find Jake and tell him she'd had enough of the party. She wanted to go home. She didn't see him outside, so she went into the house, down the heavily carpeted hallway, glancing into each room until she heard familiar voices coming from behind a closed door.

Jake spoke softly, while Fred's voice rumbled, then grew louder. His next words were clearly audible. "That boy means trouble, Jake. You're gonna have to take care of things."

She couldn't hear Jake's answer, but Fred's reply seemed to be the final word.

Julia was standing by the front door when they emerged. "Hi," she said brightly. "It's been a lovely party, but I think we should call it a night."

SHE WAS QUIET the first few miles of the drive, while Jake kept up a steady flow of talk about the party. Finally he put a question directly to her. "So tell me, Julia, how'd *you* like your first Gilmer party?"

"My first—and maybe my last," she answered.

"Now what would make you say a thing like that? You were a big hit—had every man and boy ogling you." Jake was still playing the charmer, seemingly unconcerned about what had happened.

"Jake, those men threatened Rafe. They could have hurt him, and you did nothing about it."

"Julia," he said, taking one hand off the steering wheel and reaching for hers. "I've had this job a long time, and I know how to take care of these little problems."

"I don't think it was such a little—"

"This is a very different world from yours. Come Saturday, cowboys tend to get into fights. Don't worry. You just let me handle it, honey."

Julia knew that she *was* in another world, one in which Sheriff Jake Forrester handled everything—and then had the nerve to call her "honey"! He was also still holding her hand. Somehow, she had no desire to pull away.

"I can't help worrying about them, Jake," she said, trying to distract herself from his touch. "Beth's father is so . . . protective."

"Fred loves his little girl. There's no doubt about it," Jake said. "But I guess you understand doting fathers." He looked at her with a grin. "Weren't you the apple of your daddy's eye?"

She didn't answer. "Julia? What is it?" he prodded.

"Nothing," she said softly.

"That night when we walked out on the desert and you promised to tell me about yourself, you didn't tell me everything, did you?"

She shook her head.

Jake pulled to the side of the road and turned off the engine. "Tell me now," he insisted.

"Jake, please. Why are you stopping?"

"So I can look at you and concentrate on what you're saying. Now tell me," he repeated.

"I was never the apple of my father's eye. I hardly knew him," she said. Jake remained silent. Finally she added, "He ran off and left us when I was two years old. We never heard from him again."

"But you and your mother were close?"

Julia shook her head. "She remarried. My stepfather was in the army and they traveled a great deal. He wasn't interested in kids, so I lived with my grandmother and her animals."

"Her animals?"

Julia smiled. "She had a menagerie of cats and dogs, chickens, pet squirrels. We even found and raised a baby fox."

"The beginning of your love for wild creatures."

"I guess so. They seemed so much more civilized than most of the people I knew, so much more loving and caring. Animals seldom abandon their young," she added.

Jake heard the pain in her voice, but remained silent, willing her to go on, yet afraid she'd already said more than she meant to.

She closed her eyes and leaned her head against the seat. To his surprise, she continued. "I suppose that's why I like wolves so much. They have a sense of family loyalty. All the pack—male and female—take care of the pups. They protect each other and feed each other. Did you know they mate for life?"

"No, I didn't," Jake admitted.

Julia opened her eyes then and flashed a smile—beautiful, yet vulnerable—that almost broke his heart. "I guess the two-legged wolves have given the four-legged ones a bad reputation," she said in a lighter tone.

Jake laughed and, taking her cue, pulled back onto the road. They drove to the ranch house in silence, each lost in thought.

The desert was bathed in moonlight and the air sweet with the smell of spring flowers. Jake knew he didn't want to leave Julia tonight, but wasn't quite sure of anything else. He didn't even know why he wanted to stay with her, only that he felt intense desire, combined with a need to protect her, to take all the hurt away.

He realized that he had no idea how to handle his feelings for Julia. All he could think of was kissing her, holding her. Making love to her.

Julia was trying to understand what had happened, surprised that she'd been so open. She usually didn't talk about her personal life. With Jake, whom she hardly knew, she'd already done it twice.

Yet tonight it had seemed right. She just couldn't think of Jake as an enemy. When they reached the house he switched the engine off and took her into his arms. That seemed right, too.

Julia drew comfort from his strength, falling completely under his spell from the moment his arms enclosed her and his soft, warm lips found hers. She couldn't deny the magic she felt when Jake touched her and gave herself to it, tingling with excitement.

Jake kissed his way along her neck, nibbling, tasting, licking her hot skin. He slid his fingers beneath one strap of her sundress and pulled it off her shoulder.

Julia's breast was exposed to the cool night air, then his warm mouth covered her taut nipple, his circling tongue sending sensual waves through her.

His other hand explored her calf, her knee, the back of her thigh.

"I want to make love to you, Julia," he whispered, his mouth still at her breast, his face pressed against her.

Julia felt the same, yet she held back. She'd revealed so much of herself to him, and now he wanted the rest, the most intimate part of her.

"You want it, too, don't you?" he asked, persisting.

Julia's body continued to respond to his caressing hands, yet her uncertainty persisted.

"It'll be great, I know it will," Jake said, his lips against her breast exciting her as he spoke. "It's the only way to end a night like this."

Then Julia knew why she'd hesitated. This was the way he *expected* the night to end.

She looked up and asked through the intense haze of her desire, "Is this the way it always ends for you, Jake?"

"No," he said, "I mean, sometimes, yes." He sat up beside her. "What's wrong with that, Julia? What's wrong with making it a night to remember?"

"Nothing," she answered softly. "Nothing at all." She narrowed her eyes, trying to see him more clearly in the moonlight. "It can even be a night to remember at next year's barbecue."

"That's right," he said absently, leaning toward her again.

Julia struggled with her dress, pulling it back up to restore some of the dignity she needed now.

"A night to remember at next year's barbecue," she repeated, "when I'm last year's girlfriend?"

Jake was puzzled. "I'm just talking about two people giving each other pleasure, Julia, seizing the moment."

She shook her head. "I guess I'm not a very spontaneous person. I always hold something back."

He touched her shoulder just where she'd pulled the strap up. "You didn't hold anything back when you talked about yourself tonight."

"I know," she admitted.

"If you can be open in that way, then—"

"Is that why you got me to talk about myself?" she asked.

"Of course not, Julia."

"Then why—?"

"For God's sake, I wanted to know about you, I wanted to understand your feelings."

"So you could play on them," she charged.

"Why are you so suspicious? Why are you so afraid? Why can't you let yourself get close?"

The questions kept coming; he didn't seem able to stop them, and Julia had no answers. She looked out the window at the fireflies in the desert night. She couldn't begin to sort out her emotions.

"Maybe I think too much about the consequences of being close," she said.

"What consequences?" His voice was rough with frustration.

"Rafe works for me, and obviously Fred hates both him and the project. Beth is—"

"Stop it, Julia. You're dragging half of Pierson County into this damned car. I'm only talking about you and me."

"It's not that simple."

"Of course it is," he retorted. "Your problem isn't Fred or Rafe or Beth. It's you. You can't let something good happen—and it would have been good, believe me."

"Oh, I believe you, Sheriff. I'm sure you're the best," she said scornfully, "and I'm sure all your lady friends will vouch for it."

"I'm not talking about anyone but you and me, Julia. How many times do I have to tell you that? You're hiding behind petty jealousies and ridiculous excuses. Why can't you relax and trust me?"

"Trust? We hardly know each other."

"And I guess if you have it your way, we never will," he said angrily.

"You're the one who wants one night of love, Jake. Isn't that what you said?"

He gave her tit for tat. "And you're looking for a commitment? It's not on my agenda, Julia."

She reached for the door, opened it and swung out of the Jeep without his help. Julia felt very vulnerable, but didn't let it show. "Don't worry about commitment, Sheriff. The word is not even in my vocabulary. And don't bother walking me to the door," she added, turning away and striding across the desert sand to her house. "I can damn well take care of myself."

Jake gunned the engine and wheeled out of the drive in a cloud of dust.

HE DROVE well over the speed limit all the way to Pierson City. He was utterly frustrated, angry at Julia and furious with himself. Damn the woman, getting to him like that, bringing back feelings he hadn't known in years, making him want to be protective and loving and then pushing him away.

He wasn't used to having women turn him down and insult him into the bargain. Especially when he'd been so careful. Hadn't he?

Hell, Jake couldn't remember. All he knew was that he'd been touched by all the talk about her childhood. He'd had protective, loving feelings for her then. He'd simply acted on them by holding her, kissing her. It seemed to follow that they'd make love. That was the way those things happened, wasn't it? Of course, *that* was the problem. He'd treated her just like any other woman.

Well, why should she be different? He wasn't in love with her. He couldn't possibly be in love with her. She was stubborn, independent—and overeducated.

Jake skidded to a halt in front of his house on the edge of town. He'd never bothered to grade the driveway, just as he'd never bothered to fix up the house. He hadn't planned to be in Pierson County long. That had just happened, somehow.

He couldn't say he'd really enjoyed the nights he'd spent in this house, but they'd been bearable. Tonight promised to be miserable.

He strode through the living room and into the kitchen, straight for the cabinet over the sink. He opened it and pulled down a bottle of whiskey and a glass. The bottle was still sealed, proof that he'd beaten his drinking habit. So far... With a quick, determined movement, he twisted the cap and poured himself a stiff drink. He had good reason. If he hadn't been all that happy in Pierson County, at least he'd survived this long by playing politics, being careful and doing his job.

Then in walked Julia Shelton and churned up feelings he'd thought long dead. And before he could even figure those feelings out, even though she denied it, she'd asked for some kind of damned commitment.

If that wasn't enough, Julia had brought more trouble, with her damned wolf project and her pressure on him—which she also denied—to choose sides.

On top of all that, Fred was asking the impossible, that he play both ends against the middle, spy on Julia, take care of Rafe.

"To hell with them all," Jake said and raised the glass.

Uttering a short, vehement expletive, he hurled the glass into the sink, where it shattered into dazzling shards. He stood for a moment, looking down at the broken glass and the amber liquid. Then he turned and walked into the night, slamming the door so hard that the little frame house shook.

5

THE EARLY-MORNING CALL jarred Julia from a restless sleep. She listened, hung up, and in less than ten minutes was dressed and in her car, roaring down the highway toward the Pierson County Hospital, Beth's words still ringing in her ears: Rafe had been taken to the hospital in the middle of the night. He'd been badly beaten.

Julia brought the car to a jolting halt in the parking lot and rushed toward the Emergency entrance. She was stopped there by the night-duty nurse who pointed her toward the long, green-walled corridor where Beth and Pilar waited.

"How is he?" Julia asked, gasping for breath from her long sprint. "Is he—?"

"He's all right, praise *Dios*," Pilar said, making the sign of the cross above her ample chest before enveloping Julia in a hug. "My Rafe is a strong and healthy boy."

Pilar smiled bravely, but Beth wasn't so stoic. She broke into sobs as she told Julia what had happened. "Pilar called me first, and then I called you. They beat him up, Julia. Some thugs ran his car off the road and beat him up."

"Who were they?" Julia was sure she knew the answer, even if Beth and Pilar did not.

The other women could only shake their heads.

Julia looked at Beth, then at Pilar. They seemed to be avoiding accusations, but as far as Julia was concerned, Fred Gilmer's men had gone after Rafe again, and last night there'd been no one to stop them.

Julia didn't want to bring Gilmer into it right now; Beth was upset enough. But she couldn't restrain herself from suggesting what seemed so obvious. "Beth, couldn't it have been some of the hands from your father's ranch? They seemed very upset the other night."

"I don't know," Beth said. "Maybe. I just can't believe . . ."

Pilar had her own ideas. "It was the Anglos. And this is not the first time." Head held high, she vowed, "It is only a few people, and they will not get away with what they do." She grabbed Julia's hand. "Jake has been here already. He has taken Rafe's statement. If anyone can help us, it is Jake."

Julia smiled encouragingly but remained silent. She remembered the words she'd overheard at the barbecue. Gilmer's words. *Take care of things, Jake.* She stood in the corridor, trying to comfort Beth and Pilar, yet needing comfort herself. What had Fred meant, and what had Jake's answer been?

"Can Rafe identify the men?" she wanted to know.

"No," Beth said. "They wore bandannas over their faces, and it was dark. I don't think they really meant to hurt Rafe. Just to scare him. He has a cracked rib and he's badly bruised, but they'll probably release him later today."

"Thank heaven," Julia breathed. She realized that she was trying as hard as the other two to avoid learning the truth, whatever that might be. "When can I see him?"

"The doctors are with him now," Pilar said. "That is why Beth and I are waiting. It will be a little longer."

Julia glanced at her watch. "I can wait." They sat together in the small waiting room, Beth and Pilar discussing Rafe's injuries. Julia wondered if Jake had agreed to "take care of Rafe." What did that imply? She was sure Jake hadn't personally attacked the young man. She knew him well enough to know he wouldn't have done anything like that. Maybe he'd just agreed to look the other way, help cover up whatever Gilmer's men decided to do. She didn't want to consider that possibility, either, but couldn't ignore it.

The next half hour passed slowly, but Julia was content to wait. She wanted to see Rafe and to hear what he had to say.

Beth interrupted her musings. "Julia, there's something I need to ask you—a favor."

"Anything." Julia took the young woman's hand.

A faint smile eased Beth's tense expression. "Don't say that until you know what it is."

"I'll do anything for Rafe. You know that."

"This isn't exactly for Rafe. Well, it is in a way, and for you, too, but—"

"Beth, what are you trying to say?" Julia was perplexed and a little annoyed.

"You remember how we discussed getting the community involved in the fate of the wolves?" Beth asked tentatively.

"Of course."

"Well, I guess I sort of got carried away and made a couple of commitments to talk about the program."

"Great. You don't waste time," Julia said.

"Two classes at the elementary school have decided to adopt a wolf. They're already raising the money."

"You really do work fast."

"That's not all," Beth added. "Last night at the party, one of the teachers asked me to speak at the school assembly."

"Wonderful," Julia said. "When is it?"

"This morning."

"This morning?"

Beth nodded. "It was my idea, and I know it's my job, but look at me, Julia." Her face was streaked with tears, her hair tangled. She was wearing cutoff jeans and what looked like a man's shirt. Beth, usually impeccable, was a mess. "The assembly's at ten o'clock."

Julia glanced again at her watch. It was nine-thirty.

"Julia, someone has to go, and I don't think I can...."

"Oh, oh," Julia said. "I have a feeling I know what's coming."

Beth nodded.

"Wait a minute. First of all, I don't look much better than you," she said, even though she had to admit that her khaki slacks and blouse were freshly washed. She wore no makeup, but doubted if first- and third-graders would care. "But most importantly, I don't do speeches. You know that."

"Julia, please. I'm begging you. I have to be here to see Rafe when the doctors are finished. I have to." There was desperation in Beth's eyes and voice. "Pilar needs me with her, too. Mr. Santana won't be here for another hour or so."

Julia knew she was going to agree. What else could she do? It was her project, and she'd okayed the publicity. "Don't apologize for doing your job," she said. "There's no way you can make a speech in a half an hour. I'll take over for you."

"Oh, thank you, Julia. Thank you so much."

"I should be thanking you for volunteering. Now where's the school?"

Pilar replied. "It's one block off Main Street down Sagauro. A big yellow building."

"Oh, yes," Julia said. "I've seen it. I just didn't imagine I'd ever be entering those hallowed halls, especially in this capacity."

"You'll be great," Beth assured her.

"I'll call to find out about Rafe as soon as I can," Julia said as she gave Beth a hug. "And, Pilar, tell him not to rush back to work. I can handle things."

That was a lie, but it seemed an appropriate one.

Just as she reached the nurses' station, she heard Beth call her name. "Julia, one more thing. Someone from the paper is going to cover the speech. So be eloquent!"

"No," Julia said decisively, responding to the last question. "There never has been a documented—proven—case in this country of a wolf attacking a person, certainly not a child. That's for fairy tales like Little Red Riding Hood, not for real life. No one has any reason to be afraid of wolves, especially our wolves. Next question?"

For almost an hour, Julia had forgotten about Jake and Rafe and Fred Gilmer and concentrated on the children in front of her. She'd given a brief overview of the project, trying to tone down the scientific jargon, at the same time very aware of the young reporter in the back of the auditorium, scribbling away on his pad. He looked interested, even sympathetic, and Julia hoped her intuition about him was correct.

When she'd said it was time for questions, she'd been amazed at the number of little hands that shot up. A skinny, dark-haired girl stood and spoke up, her voice high and clear. "Why do you call them Alpha and Beta? Don't they have real names?"

"Good question," Julia replied. "For scientific reasons the lead male and female wolves—the ones in charge of the pack—are Alpha, or A, One and Two. In our pack the lead wolf is a female."

The girls applauded and the boys booed. Julia smiled and went on. "But you know what? I have names for them. Very special names. My Alpha female is Saca-jewea. You all know who she was."

A chorus of young voices responded. "Right. A fa-mous Indian woman. And Alpha Two, our male, is named after Cochise. We also have Taza and Geron-imo and Pocahontas and Nokomis."

Julia knew it was time to start winding down; she probably couldn't keep their attention much longer. "I understand you're going to adopt one of our wolves. You will have the first choice, so which one—?"

"Cochise! Cochise! Cochise!" The children shouted before Julia had a chance to finish. They were evi-dently all taken with the legendary Apache Indian warrior, and Julia assured them that he would be their special wolf.

A pudgy third-grader made the presentation of money they'd collected, and Julia promised that pho-tos and a letter about Cochise's activities would fol-low.

The principal thanked Julia for speaking, and she headed out the door as the students applauded.

The young reporter caught up with her. "Great speech, Dr. Shelton. Could I get a picture for the pa-per?"

"Not today," Julia said, walking briskly to her car. "I'm in a hurry." Then she remembered Beth's lecture on the importance of good public relations. "But maybe later. Why don't you call Beth Gilmer tomorrow? She's my... my press coordinator. She'll be glad to set up photos and give you background on all the wolves."

He was clearly disappointed. "It's a fantastic story, Dr. Shelton. Kids adopting wolves. Kind of Romulus and Remus in reverse." He grinned, and Julia knew he had his lead. "I'll call Beth. We went to high school together. But I also want to talk with you. Do an in-depth story and maybe even see the wolves."

Julia nodded, climbed into the car and started the engine.

"I'd like to get into your feelings about the community's awareness of the wolf project," he continued, "especially the Cattlemen's Association."

Julia smiled in reply—and groaned inwardly as she headed back to Main Street. She was pleased by the success of her talk. Now she could concentrate on what she had to do next—confront Jake about last night and find out if he'd had a part in Rafe's beating. She hated herself for not trusting him, yet she had to ask. She had to know the truth.

"GOOD MORNING. Can I help you?"

Julia checked her headlong race toward Jake's office. His part-time secretary was on duty, a pleasant-looking blonde sitting at a desk in the outer office.

"Yes, I'm Julia Shelton and I need to see the sheriff right away." She didn't mean to sound so urgent about it. The secretary was probably thinking a crime had been committed. And she'd be right, Julia thought.

There was no need for her to call Jake. He walked over to them, looking tired and haggard, as if he'd hardly slept.

"Come on in, Julia," he said, handing his secretary a file. "Will you run this over to the courthouse, Sarah? And take your time."

"Sure, boss. I could use a break."

"I've been to the hospital," Julia said, following Jake into his office.

"Yes, I talked to Pilar a couple of times. In fact, she just called a few minutes ago. He's going home this afternoon. It wasn't as serious as they'd thought."

"But it could have been," Julia said. "They could have killed him, Jake."

His eyes turned steely. "I'm investigating, Julia."

"I heard you talking to Gilmer at the party," she blurted out.

"Oh? You were eavesdropping? You neglected to mention that, Julia."

"You knew I was there."

"And just what did you hear?" He was looking at her steadily. He didn't offer her a chair, nor did he sit down.

"Gilmer asked you to take care of Rafe."

"If memory serves me, I believe he said to take care of the situation, Julia."

"It's a matter of semantics," she said impatiently. "But whatever he asked, this morning Rafe got beaten up. What do you expect me to think?"

A muscle jumped in Jake's jaw, and Julia saw how hard he was fighting to control himself. "You think that I did it? After I took you home, I went out and beat Rafe senseless? Is that your opinion of me?"

"No, no. I didn't mean . . ." For a moment she *had* thought Jake capable of that, but only for a moment. Facing him now, she knew her doubt was unfounded. "No, not you, but Gilmer's men. I know they did it, and taking care of things for Gilmer could simply have meant looking the other way."

Jake leaned back against his desk and sighed deeply. "To tell you the truth, Julia, I'm not quite sure what it meant myself. I believed at the time my job was to see that this whole episode would blow over as quickly as possible, without anyone getting hurt."

"But someone did. Rafe got hurt, and badly. And you know who did it."

Jake put up his hand to stop the flow of words. "Julia, I have no proof. Rafe can't identify anyone. I'll talk to Fred's ranch hands, but without evidence—"

"Rafe's face is evidence," she said bitterly.

"I can't arrest the whole damn county, and I resent your thinking that I should go off half-cocked and start placing blame because of an incident at the party and a conversation you've interpreted to fit your assumptions."

"As logical as they may be."

"Logical in your mind. But you're not in charge here, Julia, I am. Let me remind you that this is the United States, where everyone is innocent until proven guilty. I can't arrest Fred's men because they got drunk and threatened Rafe. Nor can I arrest Fred because you think he's giving you a hard time about your damned wolves." He slammed his hand against the desk. "Those wolves started all of this, Julia. All the bad blood. I wish that—"

"That I'd never come here? Well, I did come." She felt her cheeks flush with anger. "But I didn't start the trouble. It has nothing to do with my wolves. Fred Gilmer started it when he broke up Beth and Rafe years ago. Well, as you say, it's a free country, and anyone can fall in love with anyone. Nobody can prevent that. Beating up Rafe isn't going to keep him away from Beth. Quite the contrary." She turned toward the door. "All Fred is going to achieve is to lose his daughter. And when you see him, tell him I said so."

Jake was about to agree with her, but with a slam of the door that made his head ache, she was gone. He ran after her, calling her name, but Julia was already in her car, driving off and not looking back.

JAKE TRACKED DOWN FRED ten miles out on the Gilmer range. He'd had a hell of a time locating the rancher, who made a habit of riding his Jeep over the miles of range he owned, checking on his cowboys, overseeing his foreman's work. Fred Gilmer didn't leave anything to chance. Jake knew that. The rancher gave orders, then made sure they were followed.

"Afternoon, Jake," Fred said, pushing his Stetson back on his head as the sheriff approached. "Didn't know you were coming to call on me."

Jake leaned against the nearby fence and looked across the range, where a herd of cattle grazed. "I think you know why I'm here, Fred."

"Let me tell you something, Jake. My family's run cattle on this land for a lot of years. My ancestors fought drought and outlaws and Indians for it. Made our spread into something special. This place means everything in the world to me."

"More than Beth?" Jake asked softly.

"You know better than that." Fred met his gaze. "Beth's my life. But you didn't come out here for a history lesson or to ask about my daughter. Get on with it, Jake."

"Rafael Santana was beaten up pretty badly last night after your party. Some of your hands had words with him earlier. I'd like to talk to them."

"Sure. You can talk to them, but I don't believe my boys would do anything like that. Hell, it was just a party, a good time. Cowboys get a little out of hand when they've had a few drinks. Nothing serious."

"Now it's my turn to ask you to level with me," Jake said. "Last night you talked to me about Rafe. You wanted things taken care of. I had my own interpretation of that request, Fred."

"I'm sure you did. And if I know you—and I think I do—it was the right one."

"Then let's say we agree. In any case, I didn't have a chance to act on it. Maybe you covered yourself and gave instructions to some of your cowboys—the same instructions, which they could have interpreted differently."

"Whoa, Jake. This is getting too philosophical for me."

"Okay, let me put it plainly. If you asked your boys to take care of Rafael Santana and they went out and beat him senseless, then you're an accessory, Fred."

Fred fixed his eyes on the horizon, shaking his head. "You misunderstood me, Jake, if you think I told my hands to follow Santana and beat him senseless...." The words hung heavily between them. "That's not my style. I thought you knew me better than that. I thought we were like brothers."

"I owe you, Fred. God knows, I've never denied that."

"And I owe you," Fred repeated. "What I meant when we had our little chat was just to talk to Rafe, cool him off. Appeal to his better nature. Let him know Beth'd be better off without him. You know, old buddy, *handle* him."

"Okay, then, that's what I thought you wanted. Problem is, I didn't have a chance. A couple of guys beat me to it."

Fred nodded. "What would you have done, exactly?"

Jake frowned. "I'm not sure. Keeping Rafe and Beth away from each other a second time isn't going to be easy."

"It's that damned Shelton woman and her wolves. Trying to change things, trying to drag us back to the nineteenth century. Well, Jake, we aren't going back. I'll guarantee that."

"I don't believe it's Julia, Fred. She and her wolves were just a catalyst. Beth knows what she wants and she's old enough to choose. She wants Rafe." Jake realized he was paraphrasing Julia's words and shifted uncomfortably.

Fred shrugged. "Beth'll come to her senses eventually. I just don't want her hurt."

"I don't want *anyone* hurt," Jake stated flatly. "So I hope Rafe can feel safe as long as he's in Pierson County."

"You have my word, Jake," Fred said easily. "And you're welcome to interview any of the boys you want."

"Much obliged, Fred." Jake knew then it was hopeless. Fred's cowboys would have alibis. They'd all stick together, and Rafe's beating would go unpunished. It made Jake angry, but he knew no way around it. What he'd told Julia was true. He needed evidence to find the perpetrators. "I'll go on down to the bunkhouse—"

"Just a minute, Sheriff," Fred interjected. "I've got a complaint."

"Oh?"

"Yep. Wasn't going to mention it, but since you're here, well, I had a calf killed last night. Pretty little thing. Looks like some kind of wild animals got it. Ripped her apart."

Jake felt a sinking sensation in the pit of his stomach. He knew what was coming next.

"Wolves," Fred said ominously. "Looks like she was torn apart by wolves."

Jake kept his voice even. "Could have been a pack of wild dogs or coyotes."

"Could've been," Fred repeated, "but I don't know of any dog packs around here, and it didn't look to me like coyotes."

"Then I'd better see the carcass. If the wolves are responsible, I'll deal with it."

"Sounds good to me. You go on down to the bunkhouse, and I'll take you around to the carcass when you're through."

FRED WALKED into the bunkhouse as Jake was finishing up his interviews.

"Got what you need here, Jake?" he asked, nodding to the cowboys who were still standing around.

They ambled out past Jake and glanced meaningfully at Fred.

"I got what I expected," Jake said when the two were alone.

"Like I told you, Jake, my boys don't go around beating up Mexican kids."

The sheriff didn't respond.

"About that carcass," Fred went on, "I'm afraid we're too late."

"Oh?"

"Yep, the boys dumped it in a lime pit and buried it over. Damn thing was drawing vultures. Guess you'll just have to take my word for it that it was a wolf job. And, Jake, you need to tell that Shelton woman this is her first warning. If it happens again, well, I can't be responsible for what the other ranchers around here might do if they get wind that wolves are terrorizing their cattle."

"Then let's keep it to ourselves for a while," Jake suggested. "There's no sense starting rumors or panic. Let me handle this, Fred."

"Sure, Sheriff. You're the man in charge."

Jake gave Fred a long, assessing look and headed toward his Jeep. He'd never felt less in charge in his life.

JULIA SLID INTO THE TUB, letting the warm water creep up over her breasts. She groaned with pleasure and began to relax. Her mad dash to the hospital had been followed by the unexpected speech and the confrontation with Jake. Her day had only grown more complicated after she'd seen Rafe and been assured he'd be all right.

She'd gotten home and checked the computer—to discover that the wolves had moved from their original site. Worried that they were getting too close to ranch property, she'd gone out to track them down in the late afternoon. She hadn't found them until twilight, when the pack had grouped to hunt.

They'd all been there, the strong and graceful Sacajewea, her loyal mate Cochise and the rest of the band. They'd looked thin but fit as they trotted across the desert, intent and focused, as if knowing exactly what they were doing. Feeling both heartened by their easy adaptation and worried that they were moving too far from their territory, she'd returned to the house too tired to do anything but take a bath.

She might have dozed in the warm water; she wasn't sure, but a sudden noise caught her attention. She sat bolt upright, listening. It had sounded like a footstep. The outer door was rarely locked, except at night when she was sleeping. It had always seemed safe on the desert. Until now.

She heard it again. There was someone walking in the living room. Julia stepped out of the tub, looking around the bathroom for some kind of weapon. Then she heard his voice.

"Julia, where are you? We need to talk. Now."

Julia grabbed her cotton bathrobe and, still dripping wet, wrapped it around her. She pushed the bathroom door shut and called, "Jake, what in the world are you doing here?"

"I came to talk."

"Well, this isn't a good time. I'm taking a bath," she told him. She didn't feel like facing him now.

"I don't care. If you don't come out, I'm coming in." He rattled the doorknob.

"All right, all right. I'm coming." She stepped out of the bathroom to face him, her heart beating against her ribs. There was something ominous about his being here; she could feel it. She could see the tension in his body and the confusion in his eyes.

"What's happened? Is Rafe all right?" That was the first thing that occurred to her, the one thing that could have brought him here like this.

"Of course," he said, sounding surprised.

Now *she* was confused. "Then why—?"

"I had to see you."

She saw him look at her and hesitated. "You could have called, Jake," she said tentatively.

"Yes, I could have," he replied, moving a step away. "But I didn't know I was coming here. I just started driving. . . ." The words trailed off, but he didn't stop staring at her. He seemed both puzzled and entranced.

He regained the step he'd yielded, then took another, drawing even closer.

Julia drew the robe across her body, all too aware that the thin cotton clung to her damp skin. Under Jake's intent gaze, she felt as though she was absolutely naked.

"I should change—put on some clothes," she began.

"No, Julia. Don't." His voice was husky. He reached out and touched her arm.

Julia looked up. "There *is* something the matter."

"Everything is the matter. Everything."

"I don't understand."

"Neither do I," he replied, taking her into his arms.

"Jake—"

"Don't ask me to explain. All I know is that I need you."

She tried to push away from him, but he held her fast in the circle of his arms. "I need you," he said more urgently, "and I didn't even know it until I saw you. Now I know." His arms tightened around her and his mouth captured hers.

She tried to turn away, avoiding his lips, but he threaded his fingers in her hair and held her, firmly at first, then more gently. The kiss deepened and Julia stopped struggling. She clung to him, her arms around his neck, answering the kiss with one of her own.

The front of her robe had opened, the sash trailing on the floor. Julia didn't care. She didn't care about anything but being held in Jake's arms and responding to the urges that were building within her. She should be fighting for control, ordering him to leave, asserting herself. But she wasn't about to do any of that. She wanted this as much as he did.

His mouth was against her ear, his voice still hoarse with desire. "Honesty, Julia. Isn't that what you want?"

She fought to understand the words she'd barely heard, then nodded.

"Well, you've got it," he said, looking down at her steadily, his hands on her shoulders. "I don't give a damn about Fred or Beth or Rafe. I don't give a damn about your wolves. I don't care about anything but you, making love to you."

He loosened his hold a little, as if to let her move away, if that was what she wanted. But Julia stood still, quiet, waiting for his next words.

"It's been like that from the first time I saw you, Julia. I knew it then, somewhere deep inside of me, and I fought against it. I think you did the same." His eyes burned into hers and Julia felt herself weaken. "Admit it," he said, "admit it, Julia." His grip on her shoulders tightened.

"Yes, yes!" The words were torn from her.

"You felt the same?" He took her into his arms again, and she clung to him almost desperately.

She whispered, her mouth against his shoulder. "I knew you were trouble. I knew I shouldn't get involved, but I also knew I wanted you here and that someday, sometime . . ."

"I'd be here?"

"Yes," she murmured.

"I'm here now," he answered. He kissed her greedily. His hands pushed her robe away and he ran his fingers up and down her back. "Like silk, Julia, your skin's like silk," he said in a tone of wonder. "I want to kiss you all over. I want to make love to you."

She clung to him as he lifted her into his arms and carried her into the bedroom. Pale moonlight shone through the window, transforming her sparsely furnished room into a surreal, glowing place for them alone.

And in that secret place he held her close and kissed her, his lips against hers, against her chin, cheek, neck, until she felt a part of him.

Julia struggled to help him out of his clothes, then caressed him as he'd caressed her, sliding her hands along his body, feeling the broad, muscular ridges of his back. She stroked his shoulders and felt hard ridges, scars. Startled, she drew her hands away.

"It's all right," he whispered. "Don't stop, please don't stop touching me."

Her fingers skimmed along his hard chest, his flat abdomen, and touched the erection pressing against her. Again she hesitated, but Jake captured her hand in his. "No, touch me there, Julia. And I'll touch you here . . . and here."

As he spoke, he slid his fingers upward, along the sensitive skin of her inner thighs to find the warmth that lay waiting for his touch. She moaned, lifting her head so that her mouth could find his. She didn't want him to stop, wanted the pleasure to be endless. She reveled in it, enraptured, as his fingers played along her body.

Jake moved his lips down her neck to her collarbone and then to the rise of her breasts. Julia gave herself up totally to sensation—the warm glow that engulfed her as he tasted the valley between her breasts, the delicious tingling that spread like wildfire along her skin as he teased a nipple with his tongue, the hot surging of her blood when his hands caressed that soft, secret place between her thighs.

She heard his voice calling her name, but it seemed far away. There was no other reality, nothing but the heat of his body against hers, his hands setting her on fire, his mouth against hers. "I want you so, Julia."

"Jake, I . . ." She meant to answer, but she'd temporarily lost all power to speak. She wanted nothing but to give herself to the passion that threatened to take control.

"Don't worry," he whispered. "I have something. I'll take care of everything."

He moved away for an instant, then returned, and somehow she knew it would be all right. Jake would make sure of that.

She reached for him and kissed him. "Make love to me," she begged. "Make love to me, Jake, or I think I'll die."

He moved over her, slipping into her welcoming softness. She stretched out a hand and touched his hair, stroked his face. What was happening between them? Their eyes met, their gazes held—and passion took charge.

6

JULIA AWOKE to the sounds and smells of cooking breakfast. It was unexpected—and delightful—mixed odors of coffee, bacon, eggs and toast. Well, burned toast.

Julia almost called out, but Jake obviously wanted to surprise her and Julia loved the idea, burned toast or not.

"Damn." She heard him curse moments later, smiled to herself and snuggled back under the covers. He'd need to try again with the toast.

Jake Forrester and Julia. It seemed impossible, yet it had happened. They hadn't planned it; they'd made love spontaneously, with an excitement and intensity she'd never known. Just before dawn they'd awakened and made love again, slowly and sleepily, until they'd drifted off to sleep in each other's arms.

The clatter of dishes and silverware brought Julia out of her reverie. Jake was setting the table. She climbed out of bed and slipped into the bathroom, glancing at herself in the mirror. There was a softness about her face, an air of contentment—not surprising, since that was exactly how she felt. Julia was both nervous and excited about facing Jake again. It had been a long time since she'd wakened and not been alone.

"Julia," Jake called from the kitchen.

She opened the door. "I'm just getting in the shower."

"Okay, but you'd better hurry. Breakfast is almost ready." His cheerful voice was a wonderful sound to wake up to, despite her vague unease. She stepped into the shower.

"WELL, GOOD MORNING," he said easily when she stepped into the kitchen. "Scrambled okay?" He acted as though it were perfectly normal for him to be in her kitchen cooking breakfast.

Julia nodded and sat down.

"I burned the toast the first time, but have a look at my second attempt."

With a flourish he put a plate before her, piled with bacon, eggs and buttered toast. "I hope you're duly impressed."

Julia realized she hadn't said a word yet.

"In fact," he continued, "you could be so impressed that you're speechless. Or maybe something else has caused the lack of communication?" He put a cup of coffee beside her plate.

"Oh, Jake, I... Thanks for making breakfast. It looks wonderful."

"'Oh, Jake, I' what?" he asked with a smile.

"I don't know what else to say."

"Then don't say anything. Just eat." He bent and dropped a quick kiss upon her lips. "Before your eggs get cold."

Julia did as she was told; then Jake, too, began eating, ravenously. Her awkwardness began to wear off.

"What's the verdict?" he asked after she'd taken a few bites and gulped half of her coffee.

"Excellent."

"Whew. I was worried there."

Julia laughed. How nice it was to have someone sharing breakfast with her! How especially nice that someone was Jake. . . .

"I'm glad you're still here," she admitted, smiling up at him.

He took her hand. "Me, too. Want more coffee?"

She nodded and he brought over the coffeepot. So *this* was the man she'd been in bed with all night; the thought of what they'd shared aroused that familiar tingling feeling. Julia's heart began to race when he sat down again.

She was gazing at him so intently, at the shower-damp hair waving across his forehead, the stubble of beard on cheeks and chin, the smooth-fitting lines of his shirt, that she missed what he was saying.

"Sorry, Jake. I didn't hear a word you just said."

"I said there's something I want to tell you."

Julia felt a sinking sensation in the pit of her stomach—something was wrong.

"Yes?" she inquired.

"Yesterday you accused me of being involved in what happened to Rafe."

"Jake, I didn't mean—"

"I know, but you were suspicious, and I don't blame you. Frankly, Julia, I'm not exactly sure what Fred asked of me or what I promised, but I talked it out with him yesterday and I feel better now. Whatever happens between Rafe and Beth is their own business. Neither Fred nor I can change it. In the meantime, it's up to me to be sure no one gets hurt again. I intend to do just that."

"Thank you, Jake." Julia felt relieved at Jake's reassurance—and a little guilty that she'd doubted him at all.

"Don't thank me," he replied sharply. "I'm the sheriff, and I have a job to do. But there's more to all this."

"I thought there might be," she said cautiously.

"Things are more complicated than they seem. I think it's time for me to explain something about Fred and me." Jake got up and began to pace.

"Jake, you don't owe me any explanations. I'm sorry you're caught in the middle of all this."

"Yeah, well, so am I, but that's how it is. And that's why I need to tell you about Fred."

"I'm listening," she said, her coffee forgotten.

"We were in Vietnam together. I was an enlisted man and he was my sergeant. It was hell on earth there, Julia. I've tried to block it out all these years, but what went on in Nam became a part of everyone who was there—and survived. None of us can ever entirely get rid of it. Sometimes, just when I think it's over for good, I have another nightmare."

"Oh, Jake," she said, sensing his pain.

"Anyhow," he went on tersely, "I was only eighteen. Fred was older, but we became friends, unlikely ones, and not just because of the difference in our ages. Fred was a rancher, a real cowboy, and I was a streetwise kid, a city slicker, I thought. But we got to know each other, the way men do under fire."

"I think I understand," she said weakly. She did in a way, but certainly not completely.

"It was close to the end, a last offensive push. Our division was right up at the DMZ—the demilitarized zone. We stumbled into a nest of Vietcong." He stopped to get his breath.

"Jake, you don't have to tell me."

"No, it's okay. Anyhow, most of the patrol was killed, wiped out. Fred was wounded, really badly, and I was hit in the shoulder. I put him on my back and started walking. Miles. God, it seemed like thousands of miles before we finally got back to our lines. They said I saved his life."

Julia got up and stood beside him, putting her arms around his waist. "You were a hero," she said quietly, moved by his words.

"No, I wasn't," he insisted. "I was just a kid in the middle of a crazy war, trying to save my buddy. He would have done it for me. Later, much later, he did save me, Julia. When I was down-and-out he brought me here. He saved my life just as surely as I saved his. Fred and I . . . what we have is deeper than blood ties. I hope I never have to go against him."

"I see," Julia said. "You're close friends, but not just because of what he did for you."

"Yes," he stated forcefully.

Julia realized that Jake wasn't hugging her back. His arms were at his sides, fists clenched. The mention of Fred Gilmer had somehow set up new barriers between them. Julia moved away and sat down at the table again. "Whether you based your friendship on what you owed each other or not, it seems to me that you and Fred have evened the score now," she said tentatively, trying not to disagree totally, trying to be fair and to understand.

"I don't see it that way, Julia," he said stubbornly. His eyes met hers. "That's what makes all this so rough."

"Why, Jake? You said yourself that what's between Beth and Rafe is their problem."

"And it is, but they're both wrapped up in this wolf thing...."

"Oh, so that's it," she said. She kept her voice calm despite her mounting anger. "Fred doesn't want me here. Well, that doesn't bother me in the slightest and shouldn't concern you. What's between Fred and me is our problem. Just like with Rafe and Beth."

Jake sat down beside Julia then, both thoughtful and concerned. "I know, but the situation between Rafe and Beth is—well, if not resolved, at least put on hold for the time being."

"And the situation between Fred and me?"

"It's more complicated."

Julia was puzzled. Something didn't add up. "What's happened, Jake?"

"Fred told me yesterday that your wolves had killed one of his herd."

"No." Her response was firm, almost abrupt. "That's not possible. I've told you, Jake, the wolves have hardly adapted to the wild. There's no way they could go after a cow."

"A calf," he corrected. "Torn to shreds, according to Fred."

"I don't believe it," she shot back. "The wolves were a little out of their habitat but not that close to his range. And I don't think they could bring down a cow."

"Calf, Julia," he corrected again. "All the wolves had to do was cut it out of the herd and then run it down."

Julia shook her head. "It's not possible."

"Well, there's no way to prove it now."

"Why not?" she shot back. "If we have more information, more facts. Remember what you said about being innocent until proven guilty? It's the same with my wolves. What kind of evidence do you have?" she asked defiantly.

"I just told you. There is no proof."

"Well, then... Wait a minute," she said suddenly. "No proof? What about the calf? Wouldn't an examination—?"

"That's the problem," Jake said ruefully. "The carcass has been buried."

Julia stood. "Ah! In that case . . ."

"Julia, you're about to sound like a lawyer."

She ignored him. "In that case it's a trick, a lie. It's Gilmer's way of getting rid of me and Rafe in one fell swoop. Well, it won't work, Jake."

Jake sighed. "Yes, it will."

"How can you say such a thing? There's no evidence!" She was almost shouting by now.

"I've tried to tell you this before, Julia. Gilmer and his buddies don't play games."

"But there's no proof, Jake," she insisted.

"It doesn't matter. If Fred's hands start spreading the word to the other ranchers that your wolves are killers, proof won't matter. All hell could break loose."

"Are you warning me again?" Her chin went up in that determined, defensive way he was getting to know so well.

Jake shook his head, partly in frustration, partly in admiration. "I'm telling you to watch your step. And I'm telling you because I care about you, Julia. Otherwise I wouldn't bother." His voice softened. "You're a stubborn, stubborn woman. And I'm damned if I can handle you." Suddenly he grinned.

"Then I'll just have to handle myself," she said, returning his grin. "I'll begin by asking for your advice. What do you suggest?"

"Caution. You can't let this happen again."

"Jake, we don't know...."

"You can't afford even the suspicion of trouble."

Julia made a quick decision. "All right. We'll move the wolves still deeper into the back country."

"That makes very good sense."

"We'll begin the move when Rafe gets back to work. It shouldn't take long to get them out of striking distance. They can only cover a certain amount of territory, and we'll make sure they're always far enough away that Gilmer's herd is safe."

Jake breathed a sigh of relief. "That sounds like a reasonable strategy." He leaned over and gave her a brief kiss, reconsidered and tried again, savoring the early-morning taste of her. "Mmm," he said. "The first kiss after the first morning coffee we've ever shared. Then the second morning kiss . . ." He reached for her again.

"Don't you have to go to work, Sheriff?"

"Eventually." His lips covered hers, and his hands found the sash on her robe. "Now, if I remember correctly . . ." He untied the sash and watched the robe fall open. "Oh, yes—"

"Jake, it's nine o'clock," Julia said weakly. It wouldn't take much more for her to forget the time.

He lingered another moment, one hand on her breast, his lips still teasing her mouth. "I'll be back," he said, "and we can pick up where we left off. Don't make any plans for tonight."

"Is that an order?"

Jake stood up, took her by the arm and pulled her up beside him. Then he kissed her thoroughly, thoughtfully and for a very long time. Julia clung to him, dazed and shaky.

"I want you, Julia Shelton," he said. "I want you very much, and nothing can change that. Now, may I ask if you have any plans for tonight?"

She shook her head, matching his playful tone. "Thanks for asking, Sheriff. It just so happens that I'm free for the evening."

"In that case, I'd be obliged if you'd allow me to call on you," he said, picking up his Stetson, swooping it low, and bending over graciously.

"Why, certainly, Sheriff," she drawled.

With a low laugh and a quick kiss, he gulped down the last of his coffee and was gone, the Jeep stirring up a trail of dust as he headed for town, the horn blaring a final goodbye as she stood at the door. His words played over in her head. *I want you. I want you very much.*

She understood words of need and desire, for she felt them, too, deeply. But she was beginning to feel something more, and that disturbed her. Was she a fool to yearn for words of love?

THE MORNING WORE ON and Julia completed her plans for moving the wolves. Problem number one was almost solved. It was close to noon when she heard Rafe's truck pull up. Beth was at the wheel.

"Problem number two," Julia said to herself as she watched Beth and Rafe get out and cross the dusty yard to the house.

"I've seen you move with considerably more grace, but you look none the worse for wear," Julia said lightly. Rafe had a black eye, bruises and a bandaged shoulder.

"I'll be back to my usual self in no time," Rafe said, gingerly taking a seat on one of the porch chairs.

"I'm in charge today," Beth announced. "He wanted to get back to work, and the doctor told him not to drive for a few days, so I finally convinced him to turn over the wheel to me. He can be pretty stubborn."

"Seems to be a trait in these parts," Julia observed dryly.

"What?"

"Nothing, Beth, nothing. I'm glad you brought Rafe back, because we have a few problems he's going to have to take care of."

"Rafe can't—"

"Beth," he said curtly but with a smile, "it's time to stop playing nurse."

Pouting playfully, Beth sat down beside Rafe and took his hand.

"What's the trouble?" he asked Julia.

She told him about the supposed wolf attack. "I don't believe it, of course, but we need to protect the pack, anyway. There's no point in taking chances."

She'd had horrible visions all morning of cowboys relentlessly tracking the wolves and ruthlessly shooting them down, cutting off their heads, as had been the custom in the last century, then displaying their carcasses for all the county to see. The thought made her ill, and she was determined to keep anything like that from happening to her wolves.

"Do you have a plan?" Rafe wanted to know.

"Yes. I worked it all out this morning. It's on the computer. I believe we can keep them at least a day away from the nearest ranch borders. That way, if they begin to move closer, we'll have time to correct their pattern. The printout's inside."

"Great," Rafe said. "I'll have a look."

Beth followed him into the tracking station. Julia put on another pot of coffee in the kitchen.

Ready to leave a little later, Rafe drank two cups of coffee. "I have the new habitat located. Shouldn't be any problem moving them out," he assured Julia.

"I'll drive," Beth decided.

Julia objected. "I'm not sure that's wise."

The young woman looked up, visibly concerned but not surprised. "I'm part of the project now, Julia."

"Yes, you're in charge of our public relations. There's no reason for you to go into the desert with Rafe."

"Because of my father?"

Julia saw Rafe look sharply at Beth.

"Frankly, yes," Julia said. "He doesn't want you seeing Rafe."

"That's our problem, Julia," Rafe told her.

Julia answered slowly. She needed to make the young people understand her feelings. "It would be your problem under different circumstances—if you didn't both work for me." She was especially careful with her next words. "I'm not accusing your father of anything, Beth, but I believe that part of his objection to our project is due to your involvement with Rafe."

Rafe answered. "You're right about that, Julia. But we can deal with it." He took Beth's hand. "It won't interfere with the project."

"Can you deal with more beatings, Rafe?" Julia asked bluntly.

As she'd expected, Beth's eyes flashed at that. "I talked to my father about the attack. He had nothing to do with it," she said flatly.

Julia diplomatically refrained from arguing. "It shows the mood of the ranchers, Beth, no matter who was responsible."

"Well," Rafe declared, "we'll just have to be sure not to give them more fuel for their fire. We'll do everything right from now on, starting with the move. And we're all in this together, Julia. We can't do without each other."

"Rafe—" she began, tempted to argue. He and Beth were still holding hands—a formidable duo, she reflected.

"You need to be here, Julia, tracking the wolves on the computer, keeping in touch with me on the two-way radio. And Beth needs to drive me."

Julia managed to get in an objection. "I have a feeling you could drive yourself, Rafe, in spite of the doctor's order."

"Maybe," he admitted, "but Beth can also take pictures today."

Beth chimed in before Julia could reply. "I have a great camera with a zoom lens in the car. I can get photos for the schoolkids, the other organizations that are requesting information—and for the newspapers."

"But—"

"I know you object to photographers getting close to the wolves," Rafe broke in, "but we'll keep our distance—and we need the photos. Everyone has to compromise a little, Julia...."

Except you and Beth, Julia thought, but before she could speak again, Beth beat her to it.

"We can't just stop the PR push now. It's more important than before. It's our lever against the enemy."

Whether or not Beth's father was one of the enemy was still to be determined, but that didn't seem to matter to her at the moment.

Rafe gave her a hug of approval. "She's right, Julia."

Julia could only nod in acquiescence. They were both right. She needed them. "Okay," she said finally, "but please be careful."

"You worry too much," he told her. "It's going to be all right. We'll check out the new site and give you a report. Then we can start the process of moving them."

"I dread that," Julia said. "I hate the idea of tranquilizing the wolves."

"Hey, Julia, it has to be done. We knew from the outset that this was a possibility. Once they're tranquilized we'll have a chance to run some tests, blood work, parasite checks. The timing isn't that bad."

"Always the optimist," Julia commented with a smile.

"We're going to succeed, Julia."

"And we'll succeed with public opinion behind us," Beth added.

"That's right. We're already generating support. Show her the newspaper, Beth."

Julia glanced over the article that the young reporter had written for the county paper. It was a well-balanced and overall favorable story with parts of Julia's speech quoted verbatim. "Well, it's not bad," she admitted.

"Sounds like you gave a great speech," Rafe told her.

"Yes," Beth agreed. "We'll have to schedule you more often."

"Oh, no. You kids can talk me into almost anything—but not that. I'm a field person. You're the PR person. Let's keep it at that. Oh, by the way, the reporter wants more info—"

"I know. He called. One of the photos will be for him." Beth glanced at her watch. "Come on, partner, we need to get going. This could turn into a long day."

BETH HAD PREDICTED correctly. It was after sundown when they called in with their final report. Julia had been at the screen most of the time, tracking their movements.

"You won't believe the shots I got!" Beth cried into the two-way radio. "One of Cochise that I'll blow up for the kids, another one of him sleeping next to Sacajewea under a rock. One of the youngest wolf—"

"Taza," Rafe broke in.

"Taza playing with a terrapin. Just like a puppy."

"Dogs are just tamer wolves," Julia reminded them. "Now I'm ready to get off this radio, so you two head back."

"On the way, we'll swing by and pick you up," Rafe said. "Dinner tonight at my folks' house."

Julia hesitated.

"You there, boss?"

"I'm here, and I think I'll stay here. Tell Pilar thanks, but I'm really beat."

"Yeah, it's hard work, sitting at that computer."

Julia heard giggles at the other end, then Rafe spoke again.

"Oh, I get it. Julia's got other plans."

"Maybe," Julia said, adding quickly, "now get yourselves home. Over and out." She switched off the radio, smiling at the sound of more giggles from Beth, turned off the monitor and walked out to the front porch.

She *was* tired; in many ways, sitting all day in front of a screen was more exhausting than working in the field. She rubbed her stiff neck and breathed deeply of the cooling night air. It would be good to see Jake.

After a short walk in the desert, Julia went back inside and sank into the tub for a hot bath, her thoughts on Rafe and Beth. Despite the impact their relationship could have on the project, Julia couldn't help but be happy for them. Love was special, something to be cherished.

She shook her head in wonder. What had gotten into her? She was sounding more and more like a romantic than a scientist. She lay back in the warm water, but that didn't help at all. In fact, it made the scientist feel even more romantic, and she began thinking of Jake.

She was still feeling that way at seven o'clock when she emerged from the tub, dried herself leisurely and dressed with more care than usual. She was looking forward to the evening; there was no doubt about that.

At seven-thirty she took two steaks from the freezer and put them out to thaw, listening for the sound of Jake's Jeep.

At eight o'clock she went out on the porch to wait.

At nine she put the steaks back into the refrigerator and made herself a peanut butter and jelly sandwich.

By ten she was concerned, and called both his office and home. No answer. Had something happened to him? By eleven she was debating with herself. Maybe he wasn't in trouble or danger and simply wasn't there because he didn't want to be. In which case she'd been purely and simply a one-night stand. Had he been playing games from the beginning, flirting with her, teasing her, ensuring that at least one of his ploys would work?

One of them had. All he'd needed to do was tell her that he wanted her, and she'd fallen quickly into his arms. She'd been warned that he was a ladies' man, but she'd ignored the comments Pilar and Rafe had made.

Fool.

Frustrated, she undressed, climbed into bed, and eventually fell asleep. She dreamed that Jake was chas-

ing first the wolves, then Julia, and that Fred Gilmer
was pursuing them all.

Then she dreamed that Jake was beside her.

"You're going to have to get a bigger bed, Julia." One
hand slid along her thigh, under her cotton gown, and
rested possessively on her hip.

It was no dream. "Jake!" She sat up.

"And from now on, lock the door. It could be dangerous for you out here alone."

"Jake . . ."

"Tomorrow I'll put on a dead bolt for you." He pulled
her down beside him.

"What are you doing here?"

"You invited me, Julia."

"For dinner," she chided.

"I'm sorry," he said, apologetically planting a kiss
upon her neck. "There was a two-car collision out on
Stage Road. Took hours to get the wrecker and tow
what was left of the cars out of the ditch."

"Was anyone hurt?"

"Amazingly, no. They all walked away, but both cars
were totaled. Reams of paperwork, measuring the skid
marks, all that. Naturally they blamed each other,
which just made the whole thing take longer."

"I guess that's what a girl has to expect when she invites the sheriff for dinner."

"Mmm." Both Jake's hands were busy roaming her
body now.

"Still, I should be angry with you for not letting me
know. . . ."

"Yes, you should be." He reached for the hem of her gown and began pulling it up.

"You could have called."

"Yes, I could have." The gown was already around her hips, and he took his time pulling it farther up, exploring with each tug.

"Stop agreeing with me." She tried to pull the gown back down.

"But you're right," he murmured. "I could have called. Except the nearest phone was twenty miles away. Of course, I could have radioed the fire chief and had him call you. Wouldn't that have been romantic?"

"I wasn't thinking romantic. . . ."

"I was. Now take this thing off," he demanded. "You don't need it."

Before she could answer, he'd skimmed the garment over her head and let it fall onto the floor.

He pulled her close, his bare chest against her breasts. "Mmm, that's more like it. Just the two of us with nothing in between."

Julia tried to keep her head clear, but it was difficult with Jake's hands playing up and down her back, the hard planes of his chest pressing against her taut, tender nipples, his teeth nibbling on her chin and cheeks.

"I've been thinking about you all day, Julia. All day. You know what I've been thinking?"

"No, but I'll bet you're going to tell me." She could feel his manhood wedged between them, hard and heavy, and shivered in anticipation, waiting, waiting. . . .

He put his mouth close to her ear and began to whisper. Julia closed her eyes, her head suddenly filled with all kinds of erotic images.

Her heart was pounding. Her whole body trembled. His words wove magic webs that surrounded, enveloped her.

"Do you know what else I've been thinking, Julia?" he asked. "It was worth the wait. Don't you agree?"

She opened her eyes and looked up at him. "Talk is cheap, Jake Forrester," she taunted. "Why don't you just show me?"

Laughing softly, he drew her to him and did just that.

7

DAWN WAS JUST BREAKING; Jake stirred, opened his eyes and planted a lazy kiss upon the top of her head. Seconds later he was asleep again. Julia chuckled to herself. He'd had a long night of work followed by a long night of lovemaking. No wonder he couldn't keep his eyes open!

But he was trying. One little move from her toward the edge of the bed and he was awake again.

"Julia . . ."

"It's still early," she said.

"Mmm."

"And you didn't get much sleep last night."

"Neither did you," he reminded her huskily.

"Well, I didn't spend half the night investigating a traffic accident. Now close your eyes and go back to sleep. I'll fix breakfast."

When she started to get out of bed, he pulled her back for another long kiss.

"Jake . . ."

"Mmm."

"Sleep," she told him a second time. "I'll call you when breakfast is ready."

"Don't call," he said drowsily. "Come in and wake me with a kiss."

"All right."

"Promise?" he insisted.

"I promise." She managed to untangle herself from his arms and plant her feet upon the floor. And by the time Julia had pulled on her robe and crossed the room, Jake was asleep again.

She made her way into the kitchen. The sun was beginning to inch above the horizon. This was her favorite time of day, and it was especially pleasant this morning. She started the coffee, humming to herself, thinking about Jake sleeping cozily in her bed.

Soon her hums turned into lilting song. Julia grinned, almost with embarrassment, even though no one could hear her. Crazy, her feelings for Jake, but wonderful, too.

The coffee was perking when she heard a sound outside. At first she thought it was the rumbling of an approaching storm, then realized it was something else. Julia went to the window to look out. Horses. Horses at six-thirty in the morning!

She pulled her robe close and went onto the porch. The sun was a bright orange, glowing directly into her eyes, making her squint.

Julia raised her hand to shield her eyes from the sun's rays. The scene before her was like something out of the Old West. Horsemen were riding across the desert toward her. There must have been a dozen cowboys packed together, riding fast. She stood entranced, disbelieving, as they pulled up. Fred Gilmer was in the lead.

"What's going on?" she cried, but got no answer, her words apparently drowned by the snorting of lathered mounts and the sounds of men's voices calling to each other.

Finally there was quiet except for the occasional stomping of a hoof and the horses' heavy breathing.

"What's going on here?" she demanded for the second time.

"Morning, Miss Shelton." Fred removed his hat.

"What do you want?" she blurted out. This wasn't a social call. Two of the riders were holding rifles; the others had them attached to their saddles. This wasn't possible, Julia told herself. It was some kind of mad dream—or nightmare.

"You know some of the boys here," Gilmer said. "Ray and Lonnie from the ranch, Buddy Silver from the Bar S and Tom Landers from the spread south of here."

Julia nodded, recognizing most of the faces. She'd met them at the barbecue, ranchers, Fred Gilmer's friends. And Jake's.

"Sorry about this intrusion, Miss Shelton. Julia. But reports about that calf killing have spread all around among the ranchers. Lots of 'em are real worried about their own herds now that it's calving time. They think the best solution is to get those wolves out of here now."

"No!" Julia almost shouted. She stepped to the edge of the porch. "The best thing to do is talk about this. There's been only one reported incident. There's no proof that my wolves killed a calf, if, indeed, one is dead."

A man spoke up somewhere behind Fred. "You saying that Fred Gilmer is a liar?"

Julia stood her ground. "I'm saying we don't know. If a calf was killed and my wolves are found to be responsible, then of course you'll be compensated."

"We don't want compensation, lady!" another man yelled. "We want those wolves out of here!"

"Dead!" someone else cried.

"Hang their hides on the fence posts, the way we used to!"

Julia's heart was racing. This couldn't be happening, not on her ranch, not in the twentieth century. She tried again. "I have data on the wolves' movements. I can prove they weren't out of their habitat."

"You can fake it, too," someone taunted.

Nothing was going to be solved this way. Julia needed time to make her case. "Please get down and come into the house so we can talk about this. I'm sure we can work something out."

Fred shook his head. "The men are too riled up for that."

She'd held her temper under control until then. "Riled by whom, I wonder, Mr. Gilmer?" she flared. "You seem to be the one who wants me out of here."

"As president of the Cattlemen's Association, I have a responsibility to speak for all the members."

His tone was calm and reasonable, in contrast to her own strained, almost panicky responses, but that didn't subdue her anger. "And I have to do what's best for me," she said. "That is to order you and these men off my property. And I mean now." She raised her chin defiantly and met Gilmer's eyes. "You are trespassing, and I demand that you leave."

For a split second she saw Fred's eyes waver, then Buddy Silver spoke up. "So you're ordering us off your property? You and who else, I wonder?"

"The lady and myself, that's who."

Jake stepped into the morning sunlight. He was barefoot, his hair tousled, wearing only his trousers. His eyes were alert, although it was perfectly obvious he'd just gotten out of bed. He was carrying a shotgun that nestled comfortably in the crook of his arm. He made no move to raise it. To Julia he was the most beautiful sight she'd ever seen.

The look on Fred's face was priceless. Surprise and dismay were swiftly replaced by anger. "Jake, what the hell—"

In two strides Jake was across the porch, edging in front of Julia to protect her.

"Where the hell did you come from?" Fred glanced around, presumably looking for Jake's Jeep.

"It's out back, Fred," Jake said. "When I heard the ruckus and saw all you fellas with guns, I figured I'd better arm myself and join the party. Now can I ask you what's going on?"

"You know damn well, Jake." Fred was back in control again. "It's those wolves. The men here heard about that killing at my place and decided it was time to get rid of those varmints for good."

"I'm afraid that won't be possible, Fred," Jake replied easily. "At least not today. You see, the lady's right. You men are trespassing on private property. You weren't invited, as I understand it. Is that correct, Julia?"

"It is," she said firmly, more confident now that Jake was here beside her.

"Since the university has leased the land where the wolves are running, that's her property, too, as I figure it," Jake continued. "If you men were to trespass and destroy the university's property—the wolves, I mean—I'd probably have to come after you."

Jake's words hung heavily on the morning air, and in spite of her confidence, Julia held her breath.

There was a brief discussion among the men. Horses whinnied, stomped, and tossed their heads. Cowboys shifted in their saddles, settling in, some of them with palms downward, as if ready to reach for their guns. For a moment it seemed to Julia as if they might break loose and charge toward the house.

Jake stared them down. Coolly, calmly, he shifted his weapon to one hand, cocking it, but keeping it pointed at the ground.

"Wait a minute there, Jake," Gilmer advised. Even though the gun was at Jake's side, the threat was real. "You're one of us. Whatever's been going on here," he continued, staring at Julia, "you know what's right."

"That I do." Jake nodded. "What's right is for all of you to ride out of here before someone gets hurt." He raised his gun slightly.

"You wouldn't shoot an old buddy, now, would you, Jake?"

"I'd arrest you. I'd arrest all of you." He looked out at the horsemen and spoke in a strong, level voice. "Buddy, Tom, Lon—all of you have better things to do with your time than hunting for wolves. So why don't you get on home, where you belong?"

Horses shuffled, men shifted in their saddles, but no one turned away.

Jake spoke again, more strongly. "I swear to you that if anyone goes after those wolves, he'll have to answer to the law. Right now I'm the law in these parts, and I don't think any of you wants trouble."

Julia saw a couple of men put away their rifles. There was still animosity, but their will to fight seemed to be waning.

"What we want is those wolves outta here," Lon called out, "and soon."

Julia spoke up boldly then. "My wolves are not here," she said firmly. "They're miles away in their habitat, which the records will show."

"Records!" Someone spat out angrily.

"Yes," she said. "And we'll be moving them even farther from civilization. We'll also begin boosting their feed, so there'll be no possibility of a problem. Will that satisfy you?"

"Whadda ya think, Fred?" another voice wanted to know.

Fred looked at Jake. "I think for now we leave the sheriff and his woman friend alone."

Julia winced at the contempt in Fred's tone. Jake started to say something, but Gilmer spoke again. "Like you said, Jake, you're the law in these parts—for now. When you come to your senses, stop by the ranch and let's talk about that. Time to start raising money for the reelection campaign, if you plan to keep on being the law. We can discuss it." Fred smiled, but it was the smile of a shark going after prey.

Jake seemed unmoved. "I'll be talking to you, Fred. You can count on that. And the next time you have a problem with Dr. Shelton or her project, I suggest you call her up, nice and businesslike, and make an appointment. The days of vigilantism are over."

"This is Pierson County, Jake, not L.A. Just remember that. We have a way of taking the law into our own hands."

"Not as long as I'm sheriff, Fred."

"We all hope that's gonna be for a long time, Jake. We really do, don't we, boys?"

There was a rumbling of voices and some laughter. Fred turned his horse. "We haven't heard the end of this," he said, facing the men. "But for today, well, we'll just see if Miss Shelton makes good on her promises."

He swung his horse back toward the house and met Julia's eyes. "If she doesn't, if one more calf dies anywhere, then no one's gonna stop us. Not you, Miss Shelton, nor the sheriff, nor the National Guard. We'll hunt down those killers, and that's a promise. Now, come on, boys, let's ride." They wheeled their mounts and rode off.

As the dust settled, Jake pulled Julia inside the house and took her into his arms. She was trembling violently. She'd been trembling all along, even when Jake had come out to stand beside her. "Thank heaven you were here," she whispered. "I was so scared."

"You did great," he said, holding her close. "You stood up to them like a trouper."

"After you got there. Before that I was a real coward."

"Like hell you were," he said. "I heard you tell Fred to get off your property."

"I was bluffing," Julia answered, gradually relaxing.

"So were they."

Julia looked up at him. "They were serious," she countered. "They had guns."

"They just wanted to see how tough you really were."

"Not so tough without you, Jake," she said. "They want to kill my wolves."

"You've known all along how the cattlemen feel."

"But I never thought it would come to this—to guns and threats."

"Come on, Julia. I think you need some coffee." He led her into the kitchen. "And what happened to my breakfast?"

"Jake, how can you think of breakfast at a time like this?"

"I'm hungry." He poured coffee and handed her the bowl of eggs she'd left on the counter. "Scramble," he demanded. "I'll try not to burn the toast this time." He lighted the old-fashioned oven.

Julia started beating the eggs, then it hit her. "Oh, Jake. You're in big trouble, too. The look on Fred's face when he saw you . . ."

Jake shrugged. "It doesn't matter."

"But it does," she insisted. "Didn't you hear what he said about your campaign?"

"Fred won't be running for sheriff next election. I will."

"But he heads up your election campaign. And he's your friend, your best friend. Or he was." Julia thought of what Jake had said about his friendship with Fred. Her project could spoil all that for him.

"I'll take care of it, Julia," he assured her. "Besides, that's not the most pressing problem at the moment. Our wolves are top priority."

Our wolves. The words filled Julia with warmth and hope.

"You're right," she said. "I'll get in touch with Rafe, and we'll start making plans. It's not going to be easy. We'll have to move them farther than we planned. They're almost at the limit of our tracking equipment now."

Suddenly she had an idea. "Maybe I won't have to move them. I've recorded everything. I have the data. I could prove—"

"Julia," Jake said warningly. "I doubt if the ranchers would believe anything you told them."

"But I have it all on the printouts."

"They're acting on emotion and years of prejudice, not logic. You don't have any choice."

Julia's spirits sagged. "I guess it's about as bad as it can get. The ranchers think the wolves are killing calves. Fred is furious because Rafe is seeing Beth. Now your job is in jeopardy because you and I are...are..."

"Intimately involved," Jake finished with a smile.

With an effort, Julia smiled back and managed to contain her pessimism. "From now on, things can only get better."

THE NEXT DAY Julia, Beth and Pilar were sitting at a small table at the back of the grocery store drinking coffee and sharing a plate of pastries. Beth was going over a list of activities and fund-raisers she'd planned for the Save Our Wolves Project, but Julia couldn't raise any enthusiasm. She'd spent hours on plans to move the wolves and still hadn't been able to solve the logistical problems.

"Look at all this, Julia. It's great. I don't know why you're so negative about it," Beth said.

"I'm not negative, Beth. I just have a lot on my mind."

"Everything's going to work out," Beth said optimistically. "Especially after what Pilar has done. She's coordinated a carnival at Our Lady of Hope Church and convinced the high school to donate proceeds from the senior class play to adopt Sacajewea, and—"

"I know. You've done a great job, Pilar," Julia said.

Pilar flushed with pride. "And just look at the publicity Beth has gotten for us," she said, clearly wanting to shift attention away from her own achievements.

On the table beside Beth was a sizable pile of newspaper clippings about Julia, her hope of returning the Mexican brown wolves to their natural habitat, and the community's involvement.

Beth spoke up again. "It really started with the schoolchildren's adoption of Cochise. That grabbed the headlines and was the hook that most of these stories went after."

"I'll admit the publicity is going well," Julia said. "But this . . ." She picked up a telephone message that Beth had given her. "This kind of thing is your job, Beth, not mine. No way am I going to Los Angeles to be on some talk show."

Beth's eyes widened. "But, Julia, Polly Anderson has one of the top shows in the country," she said in audible dismay. "Most people would kill to get on *Anderson in the a.m.*"

"Not *this* 'people,'" Julie retorted. "Anyhow," she asked suspiciously, "why does she want me?"

"Because," Beth explained, "I went to college with one of her assistant producers, and I've been bugging her every day with information and pictures and phone calls about you and the project. She thinks you're a very interesting lady, so when they had a guest cancel for the day after tomorrow, Tiffany called me. This is a big deal, Julia. You have to go."

"I can't." She hadn't told Beth or Pilar about her early-morning visitors and didn't plan to. Not yet. "You go."

"They want *you*," Beth insisted, "not me."

"It's impossible," Julia declared.

Pilar had been listening quietly. Now she spoke up. "Nothing is impossible for you, Julia. We all know that. Los Angeles, it is not that far away. Just an hour or two by air."

"Pilar . . ." Julia began threateningly.

Beth jumped in again. "Ten minutes on the Anderson show can reach millions of people. The more who know about the wolves, who want to adopt one, the safer they'll be. Think about Taza and Nokomis. No one has adopted them yet."

An image flashed into Julia's mind of the ranchers, their guns slung menacingly across their saddles. Words came back to her. *Hang their hides on fence posts.*

"I know you're right about the show," she said slowly. "It could reach lots of people, but now is a very bad time. I've been thinking about moving the wolves even deeper into the desert. . . ."

"But the site Rafe and I scouted was perfect."

"I believe it would be safer to get them even farther from civilization," Julia hedged, still determined not to tell Beth what her father was up to. "I've already called the university and told them my plans. We may have to boost up the computer's tracking powers."

"But I don't understand," Beth said with a frown.

"My Rafe can help," Pilar said suddenly.

"I'm counting on him," Julia answered, relieved.

"I'm available, too," Beth chimed in.

"It's a big job," Julia went on. "I don't know how I can leave. . . ."

"Then we must ask Luis and Rafe's brothers. Even I can help," Pilar said, reaching out with her warm, plump hand to grasp Julia's. "That is what families are for, Julia, to help each other. You are our family, too."

Julia felt a sudden sting of tears, which she blinked back. She was beginning to feel cornered. Finally, she gave in. "Okay, okay. I can't fight both of you. I'll go to Los Angeles, but only for a day."

She saw Pilar and Beth look at each other and smile triumphantly. Julia couldn't help smiling, too, as she thought about Pilar's words. It felt good to be part of a family at last.

"I CAN'T BELIEVE I'm going to L.A. *now*," Julia muttered as she and Rafe pored over a topographical map. "Just when everything is such a mess."

"It's the best time," Rafe countered. "It'll take me a couple of days to find a new spot that's far enough away to satisfy the ranchers and still close enough for us to monitor. By the time you get back, we'll be ready to move. You won't miss any of the excitement, Julia."

"I know, but—"

"Trust me," he admonished. "I can handle it."

"With my help and the rest of the Santana family," Beth declared, looking up from the press release she was typing at a makeshift desk in a corner of the office. "I'm sorry about what happened yesterday morning, Julia."

"What?" Julia played dumb.

"It's all over town."

Of course. It would be, Julia realized. She'd sworn Rafe to secrecy, well aware that Beth would eventually find out.

"I've already told Daddy what I thought about that stupid scene from the Old West he pulled. I just can't believe it."

Julia was silent. To her, Fred Gilmer's behavior didn't seem out of character at all.

"I guess your working with us has put you at odds with your dad," Rafe said.

Julia frowned, surprised that Rafe didn't seem to be aware that he was part of the problem, too.

"Daddy and I haven't agreed on anything in years, starting with where I should go to school, what I should major in, and who I should date. And he really has no say-so about where I work, either. But we still love each other. We just argue a lot," she added with a shrug. "Daddy thinks he knows what's best for everyone."

Julia remained silent.

Beth continued, partly in defense of Fred, Julia thought, and partly in explanation. "Daddy still has a cowboy macho image of New Mexico. He never would have hurt you, Julia."

Julia struggled to formulate an appropriate answer, finally saying, "It was pretty scary, Beth."

Then Rafe broke in, trying to placate her. "Most folks in these parts have guns, Julia."

"That doesn't mean I have to like them."

For a long, uncomfortable moment, there was complete silence. Then Beth pulled her press release from the typewriter and handed it to Julia. But the subject was still unresolved. "He's not so bad, Julia," Beth said anxiously. "I had a long talk with him about the wolves, and I gave him some of our literature to read. I'm sure in time he'll understand the importance of our project. The wolves belong here, just as much as the cactus and the mountains belong."

Julia managed to avoid replying while she read the press release. She was touched by Beth's loyalty to her father, but couldn't imagine that he'd be moved by articles about the wolves. Everything seemed to be slipping from her control. Even the trip to California wasn't her idea. All she could think about was getting it over with and returning to the wolves.

Jake arrived at sundown, and at the familiar sound of his Jeep, Julia felt her pulse quicken. Just knowing he would be with her seemed to make everything easier.

She went to the door to meet him, and when he leaned down to kiss her, she lifted her lips to his, not caring that they weren't alone.

The four of them cooked dinner together, throwing hamburgers onto the grill. Rafe and Julia took turns watching the wolves' movements on the computer. It wasn't until they'd all settled down for coffee that they persuaded Julia to talk about the L.A. trip.

"So you're heading for the big city," Jake said. "Where're you staying?"

Julia looked at Beth questioningly. She hadn't asked.

"The station is putting her up at the Beverly Hills Hotel," Beth said.

"Hmm. First class," Jake observed. "It takes me back."

Julia wanted to ask him if he would go with her, but didn't—not in front of Rafe and Beth.

"Are you nervous, Julia?" Rafe wanted to know.

"About the TV show? Scared out of my mind," she said honestly.

"You'll do great," Beth assured her. "Polly Anderson is a doll, or that's what Tiffany says. Not confrontive at all. She's into ecology and conservation, so it ought to be a piece of cake for you. Just tell her some whimsical stories about the wolves."

"Yeah, like how they eat calves," Rafe piped up.

"Oh, you," Beth said, going around to stand behind Rafe's chair. "We need to get going. Julia's had a long day."

Rafe got up and slipped his arm around Beth's waist. "At my last check on the computer, the wolves were out near Apache Rock. Want to take a look in the moonlight, Beth?"

Beth met his eyes dreamily, and they left.

"THEY'RE REALLY IN LOVE, aren't they?" Julia said softly as they walked on the cool desert sand.

"And not afraid of one damn thing," Jake mused. "That boy's ready to take on the world."

"And she's ready to stand by him," Julia added.

"A formidable pair." Jake took her hand. "But not the only young lovers who want to see the desert by moonlight."

"Not so young," Julia reminded him.

"Who, us? Of course we are."

She looked at him and grinned.

"Well, we're lovers, nevertheless."

Lovers. The word was at the same time comforting and disturbing. She and Jake shared a bed and the most intimate part of themselves, but Beth and Rafe were *in love.* That indicated something deeper, a commitment and a future. Julia wasn't sure Jake and she had that, not yet, anyway. She wondered if they ever would.

"Did you talk to Fred today?" she asked as they topped a rise and looked across the vast, still, expanse of the desert, silvery in the light of the moon.

"Nope."

"Jake..."

"It'll be all right, Julia, when Fred cools off."

"I wonder if that'll ever happen."

"It will. I know him pretty well."

"That's the problem." She turned to face him. "Your friendship with Fred was so close until I arrived and ruined it for you."

Jake put his fingers to her lips. "You could never ruin things for anyone, Julia, and this has nothing to do with friendship. I was doing my job. Fred and the other cattlemen were trespassing."

Of course. He hadn't been doing it for her. He'd protected her against trespassers, just as any law officer would have done. "I just hope doing your job won't mean losing your job, Jake," she told him. "Your life here depends—"

Again he silenced her. "Not tonight, Julia. I want to forget Fred and the cattlemen and my job."

"Okay," she said, putting her arms around his waist. "Let's seize the moment, then."

"Are you seducing me, Julia?"

She stood on tiptoe and kissed him, pressing her body close, moving her hips against his, playfully, suggestively. "The night is young," she murmured against his lips, "and the kids have gone."

"Thank heaven for that. I wondered if they'd ever leave."

"We have the house all to ourselves."

Jake's arms tightened round her, and she could feel the strength of his arousal as he returned her pressure. "Your bedroom is much too faraway," he whispered.

"What do you suggest?"

Julia wasn't prepared for his answer. He stepped out of her arms, unbuttoned his shirt and pulled it off. With a grand gesture, he spread it on the ground.

"Here?"

"Haven't you ever made love under the desert moon?" he teased.

"What do you think?" She shivered a little in excitement as he undid the buttons of her blouse, brushing his fingers against her breast.

"I think it's time you went back to school, Doc." He slipped her blouse off and placed it on the ground beside his shirt.

"But the sand...and things," she protested halfheartedly, but he simply stripped off his trousers, added them to the other clothes and lowered her onto the makeshift couch.

"You'll be so busy with me, you won't notice any of those 'things,'" he said. Jake kissed his way along the column of her neck, stopped to nibble on her collarbone and then moved to the hollow between her breasts.

"You're beautiful in the moonlight," he whispered, "soft and vulnerable."

"So are you."

He laughed at that.

"Really, you're beautiful, too." The moonlight shone upon his tawny hair and softened the strong planes of his face.

"Men aren't beautiful!" he protested.

"You are." She took his face between her hands and kissed him lovingly, deeply, darting her tongue in and out of his mouth, tasting and savoring.

"Oh, Julia, what you do to me," he murmured. He caressed her breast with his fingertips through the lacy fabric of her bra, then found the hardened nipple with his mouth. His tongue circled her nipple, and the lace rubbed against her breast. His warm hands moved across her skin. Julia squirmed beneath him, aroused, digging her fingers into the muscles of his back. She closed her eyes, whispering his name again and again.

"Jake, oh, Jake."

"It'll only get better," he promised. He unsnapped her bra and tossed it aside, then pulled down her khaki shorts. He left her silky bikini panties on and rubbed his fingers against the soft fabric between her legs. Julia arched against his hand, seeking still more pleasure.

He leaned over and kissed the inside of her thigh, tracing lazy patterns with his tongue until he found her moist center.

The pleasure had grown intense, was almost too much for her, and Julia tried to pull away. She didn't want to surrender to him yet. But Jake continued to hold her, love her, send wave after wave of sensation shimmering through her until she was on fire for him, her skin hot and flushed in the cool desert air.

"Jake..." She tried to hold back, but it was impossible. Crying out, holding on to him with all her strength, she let passion take over. Falling back, sated at last, she murmured, "I meant to—"

"Don't worry. It's not over yet."

"Jake, I—"

"Don't worry, Julia," he said huskily. "I told you that it's not over."

He slid one hand down her arm and caught her hand in his, guiding her fingers to where his need was greatest. She felt his erection and caressed him.

Somehow, magically, her own arousal returned. "I didn't think..."

"Don't think," he said, "only feel."

She did just that, pulling him close against her. His back was hard and strong, his body poised above her.

"Do you want me now, Julia?"

"Yes, yes," she urged, taking off her bikini with his help.

Then he filled her, and they met as equals.

His thrusts were long and deep; she held on to him, wrapping her legs around his back, clasping him to her, wishing for the moment when they would be one.

It happened unbelievably quickly. Waves of ecstasy rushed through her. She opened her eyes and saw the moon shining, its white light intense and powerful.

Jake still held her, his heart pounding, his breathing just as ragged as hers. Neither of them spoke; he covered her with his shirt and she snuggled close. There was much she wanted to tell him—that she felt bound to him by their act of love, thought of him constantly and wanted him desperately. That she loved him. But she held the words back, afraid to speak, to spoil the beautiful moment.

He kissed her shoulder and wrapped the shirt around her. "Can't have you catching a chill, can I?"

"I'm not cold," she said. "I've never felt so warm."

"Just the same, I'm going to take you inside. Who knows what might happen once we get into bed?"

"Oh, Jake, no. We couldn't."

"Who says?" He got up, pulled her to her feet and gathered up their clothes.

Silently they walked toward the house, naked, exchanging kisses and wrapped only in moonlight.

8

JAKE WAS DRIVING Julia to the airport early the next morning, listening to her long list of orders to be passed on later to Rafe and Beth. Finally he chuckled and said, "You've already told them, Julia. You wrote everything down and went over it. Twice. They know what to do."

"You're right," she admitted, "but I'm jumpy about leaving the wolves just when they have to be moved, and—"

"Going on the TV show," he finished for her. "That's what it's all about, isn't it? You'll be back in twenty-four hours, and the wolves will survive nicely. But will you survive *Anderson in the a.m.?*"

"No!" she declared nervously.

Jake took his hand off the wheel long enough to give her arm a squeeze. "Of course you will. You'll be a hit, you and your wolves."

"It's not me and my wolves. It's just *me*."

Jake laughed again. "I'd like to see you bring the wolves onto Polly Anderson's show."

"They'd be great."

"So will you," Jake said seriously. "You're a people person, Julia. Whether you admit it or not. Look how well you did at the school."

"Jake, those were kids."

"Kids are people," he reminded her. "Think of it like that, and you'll be fine."

It was impossible. There was no way Julia could compare talking in front of first- and third-graders with appearing on network television. She watched the sun-baked scenery roll by, trying not to think about what lay ahead.

Jake continued to encourage her with his quips, but it didn't work. Only one thing would help. "Why don't you come with me?" she asked.

"What did you say, Julia?"

Of course, he hadn't heard her. The words she'd been thinking since last night had been barely audible. She tried once more. "You could come along," she suggested, attempting to sound casual.

Jake just smiled.

"I mean it, Jake," she said. "You could hold my hand through the Polly Anderson torture and then show me the town. You know L.A."

"Oh, yes, I know L.A.," he replied. "And it knows me. But I doubt if anyone I used to know there would be interested in seeing me, even though I'm cleaned up, and frankly I don't have the slightest interest in seeing them."

Jake didn't want to relive old memories. Julia understood that. Still, it would only be for a day, so she persisted. "We wouldn't even have to go out."

"Julia, I'm not about to venture into the City of the Angels, for one hour, let alone twenty-four."

Her expression must have given her away, because he slowed down, leaned over quickly and kissed her on the lips. "You understand, don't you?"

"Of course." She was still disappointed.

"Then don't pout," he advised. "And thanks for the invitation, Doc. We'll take a trip together sometime."

He might as well have been talking to a child, telling her not to pout, promising another trip. She understood him; why couldn't he understand her and her needs?

That question plagued her throughout her flight. She'd expected more from Jake, and he'd been able to give nothing except a glib reassurance, leaving her hurt and lonely.

The flight was bumpy and the food terrible. Julia reflected that Jake had his own problems and concerns, and she couldn't expect to be at the top of his list. Even though he'd gone to bat for her against Fred Gilmer, by his own admission it had been out of duty to his job, not devotion to her.

Yet she simply needed him, wanted him to be with her, to hold her hand through all this. Julia, who never depended on anyone, needed Jake now; Julia, who was always rational, was giving way to irrationality.

That bothered her, but she hardly had time to worry about it; the pilot announced that they were approaching Los Angeles International Airport. She tightened her seat belt and swallowed hard. Her nerves had been frayed by the rough flight and from anticipating the day ahead.

The intercom went on again.

"Ladies and gentlemen, it looks like there'll be a slight delay in landing. No real problem, just heavy traffic. We're in a holding pattern, and I'll let you know as soon as I receive permission to land."

That was all she needed, Julia thought. It wasn't even possible to *get* to L.A. without feeling frazzled. She could just imagine what she'd be like by the time she finally reached the hotel, let alone the TV studio.

TIFFANY, a young production assistant, Beth's friend, met her when the plane finally landed. They'd stepped onto the longest escalator Julia had ever seen, when Tiffany said, "The show's been delayed, but only until tomorrow."

"You're not taping until tomorrow?" Julia was dismayed. "I really can't stay over that long."

Tiffany tossed her long, dark-blond-streaked hair around a few times and ran her fingers through the strands. "The delay won't cause a problem," she said brightly.

"Maybe not for you, but it will certainly cause a problem for me."

They'd reached the ground level. Julia followed Tiffany to the baggage claim area. "I have responsibilities. They can't be ignored!" Julia protested.

"It'll only be a few more hours than planned," Tiffany assured her, adding sincerely, "I'm terribly sorry, but these things happen."

"What things?" Julia stopped walking.

"Polly has an awful sore throat. I mean, terrible. She can hardly talk above a whisper."

"Well, I'm sorry to hear that, but—"

"You know how it is with two shows a day and so many public speeches."

Julia didn't know, nor did she care to find out. *If*— and it was a big if—she made this appearance, it would be her last one. From now on, Beth would be the spokesperson.

"Polly's poor vocal chords just gave out," Tiffany continued. "Honestly, it was terrible. She's so upset about the postponement."

"Well, she's not the only one."

"We expect by tomorrow she'll be fine."

"What do you mean, *expect?* You just said you were definitely taping tomorrow."

"Well, I'm certain we will," Tiffany assured her. "Polly has the best doctor in L.A., in the world, for that matter."

"I don't doubt it."

"Tops in his field," Tiffany went on. "And he gave her shots, you know, antibiotics, everything, and said all she had to do was keep quiet for the next twenty-four hours." Tiffany flashed another smile. "Problem is, Polly's not so good at keeping quiet."

Julia wasn't amused.

"But don't worry, she'll follow orders."

"How can you be sure?" she asked.

"Because she's invited a special audience for your show. Polly won't want to let them down. Besides, the promos are already running."

That, Julia suspected, was the real reason. Show business. It was just another kind of *business*, as she'd often heard.

"You'll still be leaving tomorrow, just a few hours later," Tiffany reminded her. "But if you'd rather not fly back right after the show, we've held your room for an extra night. Our expense, of course," she added. "You might like to have a night on the town."

"I don't think so," Julia decided.

"But you will stay overnight for the taping?"

"You have me—" she looked at her watch "—for another twenty-four hours. No longer." Julia didn't mean to be demanding, but she wasn't about to stay any longer than that. She was involved in a serious project, and no amount of publicity would help if anything happened to her wolves. They were *her* responsibility. Besides, she didn't think she could stand the suspense and nervous anticipation for much longer than that.

"Great," Tiffany said. "I'm so relieved, and I know Polly will be, too. Now, which is your luggage?"

"Tiffany," Julia said, "I'll only be here overnight. *This* is my luggage." She indicated her large carry-on bag.

"Omigod!" Tiffany was visibly appalled. "Well, it's all right. The hotel shops carry just about everything. Feel free to get whatever you need and charge it to your room. Of course, we'll also have hair, makeup and wardrobe on the set."

"My, that's a relief," Julia said with a wry grin. Even if she was a disaster on the show, her makeup and hair would be perfect.

Tiffany drove from the airport to L.A. in what Julia suspected was record time, defying all rules of safety.

"How do you manage to avoid getting tickets?" Julia asked as they pulled into the hotel driveway and left the car for valet parking.

"Just careful driving, I guess," Tiffany said, carelessly tossing her blond locks. Julia laughed, beginning to enjoy herself.

After depositing her hopelessly inadequate luggage in her room, Julia followed Tiffany into the famous Polo Lounge, where she tried a vermouth *cassis* that Tiffany recommended.

Julia discovered that she was starving, so Tiffany ordered a delicious lunch for them. Halfway through the meal, Tiffany excused herself and, Julia assumed, went off to the powder room.

She'd been gone a couple of minutes when a waiter arrived carrying a telephone, which he plugged into the booth. "Phone call for Dr. Shelton."

Julia picked up the receiver. *Was something wrong?* But Tiffany was giggling on the other end of the line. "I just thought you should get used to feeling like a star."

Julia didn't exactly feel like a star, but laughed at Tiffany's stunt. After lunch, they window-shopped on

Rodeo Drive, sipped cappuccinos at a sidewalk café and lounged by the hotel pool. By the end of the day, Julia had relaxed.

"Now, about tonight," Tiffany said when they returned to the room, "I think you should take in some of the nightlife, and I have the perfect escort...."

"Enough, Tiffany," Julia declared. "I don't want to do anything but relax, soak in a warm bath and get a good night's sleep."

"That sounds terribly boring."

"Not to me. You've been a wonderful hostess. I never expected such grand treatment, but I think it's time for a rest."

"I promised Beth I'd entertain you, but if you're sure..."

"I'm sure."

"Not even a taste of the nightlife? My boyfriend and I would come along, of course."

"Not even a taste." Julia was very sure.

"Well, just so you don't spend your time worrying about the show."

"I won't," Julia promised.

Tiffany held out her hand. "Then good luck, Julia. It's been great fun, and I'm sure you'll wow 'em tomorrow."

The minute the door closed, Julia realized where she was, what she'd been doing all day, and was appalled. Appearing on television was totally out of character for her, but running around Beverly Hills with a production assistant named Tiffany and actually having enjoyed herself was even more farfetched.

All the same, she'd managed not to think about the show tomorrow—and the fact that Jake wasn't here to share it with her. That was the real problem. Without him she felt helpless.

"Damn," she said. "Why did I get myself into this?" Mumbling "Never again, never again," she headed for the bath.

By the time she'd dried off and donned the hotel robe, she'd decided to work and put everything else out of her mind.

Seated at the desk in her suite, Julia pulled out an article she'd been working on for the university journal and settled comfortably into the world of academia and *lupus canis*, where she really belonged. She ordered dinner from room service and managed to complete the article to her satisfaction.

It was still only eight o'clock. Plenty of time for the butterflies to begin again. To avoid them, she picked up the phone. She wanted to call Jake. He was the one she needed to talk to. She missed him terribly, but couldn't bring herself to call and tell him so. Instead she dialed home.

JAKE HAD MEANT to have dinner in town, but when he got into the Jeep and started down Main Street, he found himself driving past the café and heading for the highway.

He pulled up in front of the adobe house just as Rafe and Beth were taking a steak off the grill.

"Come on in," Beth called. "You're just in time for dinner."

Jake tried to pretend he'd eaten, but they clearly didn't believe him for a minute.

"You look like a hungry man to me," Beth said, setting another place at the kitchen table.

"And there's plenty for everyone," Rafe said encouragingly.

That was all it took. Jake wanted company. Not only that, he admitted to himself, he also wanted to be with someone close to Julia.

He thought they'd never get around to talking about her. He had to listen to all the details of Rafe's day at the computer, going over the tapes of the pack's movements, and looking for new sites. Then he had to look interested in Beth's lineup of speeches for the week.

"I have a school over in the next county that wants to adopt Taza," Beth said. "Julia was really excited."

Finally some mention of Julia. "When did that happen?" Jake asked.

"This afternoon, while Rafe was on the computer. I went over to—"

"Then how could Julia know about it?" That was what really interested him.

"Oh, didn't we tell you?" Rafe asked. "She called."

"When?" Jake couldn't help being a little annoyed that she hadn't called him.

"Not long before you got here," Rafe said, taking a bite of the steak. "This is done just perfectly, if I do say so myself," he added.

"Never mind the steak. What did Julia say? How'd the taping go?"

"It didn't."

"What?" Jake put down his fork and glared at Rafe. "Let's get some facts here, Rafe."

"Okay, Sheriff," Rafe said with a grin. "The big honcho, What's-her-name Anderson, has the sniffles or something. They aren't taping until tomorrow afternoon, so Julia won't be back until late tomorrow night."

"And you didn't bother to tell me?"

"I didn't think it mattered. I was planning to pick her up, anyway, since you'd be working."

"But I won't be working tomorrow *night*," Jake reminded him. "What time's the flight?"

"Dunno," Rafe said.

"Rafe—"

Beth chimed in again. "They thought she might want to spend tomorrow night in L.A., so I guess they hadn't booked a flight. She'll call again after the taping."

"You guys *are* full of information," Jake said, "as long as somebody pulls it out of you. And the steak's too well-done, by the way," he added with a grin. "Now, what else did Julia say?"

"Do you think we should tell him?" Rafe asked Beth.

"I think we'd better, so he'll be prepared."

"All right, you two . . ."

Rafe laughed. "It's nothing, really. We just mentioned that the story was all over town about you running out on the porch half-dressed the other day."

"Great."

"Well, it is, Jake," Beth said.

"I know, but you didn't have to bring it up with Julia."

"She might as well know now, so she'll be prepared. Besides—" Beth smiled "—I think it's very romantic. It adds to your legend...."

"Wait a minute—" Jake began.

"And it makes Julia kind of glamorous," Rafe interrupted.

"I doubt if she agreed with that."

"No, she didn't, actually," Rafe admitted.

"What time did you say she called?"

"I told you, Jake. Maybe a half hour before you got here."

Jake looked at his watch. "About eight o'clock?"

Rafe nodded.

"It's nine-thirty now."

Rafe nodded again and Beth stifled a giggle.

"She's probably still awake, don't you think?"

"I imagine so," Rafe said.

"Well, thanks for the dinner, kids. I'll be going now. Sorry to eat and run." Jake got up, taking his plate to the sink.

"You can use the phone here," Rafe offered.

"Thanks, but I'll just go on home."

IT WAS ALMOST TEN O'CLOCK when the phone rang in Julia's suite. A little thrill of excitement ran through her when she heard Jake's voice.

"Hi, Doc," he said casually. "I hear there's been a hitch in the plans."

"Rafe filled you in?"

"He did. In fact, I just had dinner out at your place. Beth's there, too, full of news about one of the schools that's adopted Taza, and Rafe went on about the new site he'd found for the wolves, deeper in the desert with an underground stream and spring, lots of rocks for a den, all that."

"I know," Julia said. "They told me all about it."

"What I really wanted to hear about was you," Jake said. As soon as the words were out he began to feel foolish, like a teenager in school. What the hell was happening to him, he wondered—driving past the café, going to Julia's house, with nothing in his mind except her? That wasn't like him. None of this was like him.

Julia felt again the little thrill of excitement. Even if he wasn't with her, at least he'd called, at least he was thinking about her.

"Are you feeling better about the taping?" he asked.

"Now I am," she admitted. "Now that I hear your voice. I really miss you, Jake."

"I miss you, too, honey," he said, adding quickly, "but tell me how you like L.A."

"To be truthful, I had an enjoyable afternoon with a production assistant from the show. Her name is Tiffany. She actually was a lot of fun. Took my mind off the taping, at least for a while. Took my mind off you," she added, "and how much I miss you."

"Same here," Jake said. "It's gonna be awfully lonely in bed tonight."

"It's not just that," Julia told him. "There's more." She paused, searching for the right words. "You and I don't talk much about our feelings. I guess we haven't had a lot of practice."

Jake was silent, so Julia plunged on. "I need you as my friend, Jake. I've begun to depend on you. I guess you didn't expect to hear that from me."

"No, I didn't," he said. "You've always been so darn independent and in control."

"Maybe I'm changing."

"Maybe."

He fell silent again.

"Jake . . ."

"Julia, it's not easy to talk about these things on the phone."

"I know."

"Maybe when you get home . . ."

"Yes," she said quietly.

"Let me know when your flight gets in, and I'll pick you up."

"No, Rafe is going to—"

"We'll see," he interrupted. "Just call as soon as you know the time."

"All right."

"Now get some sleep, Julia."

"I will."

"And good luck."

The call only made Julia feel worse. She'd hoped to talk about her feelings over the phone, since she never had the nerve when they were together. But it hadn't worked. Would she ever be able to tell Jake what she wanted to say? That she was in love with him?

JAKE LEANED BACK on the bed, cursing himself. He'd been thinking about Julia ever since she left, and there'd been so much he'd wanted to say to her. In the end he hadn't said any of it. Hell, he should be there in L.A. with her. He wanted to be there. It just wasn't possible.

His fears about the past kept him prisoner, made him powerless to be there with her. What if he'd gone when she'd asked him yesterday on the way to the airport? Would the pull of the past have been stronger than the reality of the present? Now he'd never know.

Jake got up and began to pace the floor of his small bedroom. He'd begun a new life in Pierson County, and even that life appeared pretty precarious at the moment. He and Fred were on the outs, and his association with Julia certainly hadn't raised his standing with the Cattlemen's Association. He needed to stay home and mend some fences, not go running off to L.A. because Julia needed him, even if he knew deep down that he needed her, too.

JULIA'S THOUGHTS were not on the television show but on Jake when she awoke. Why had she chosen this time of her life to depend on a man, and why did the man have to be Jake Forrester, who'd let her know from the beginning that long-term relationships weren't in his nature? A phone call from Tiffany distracted her. Polly was ready. They'd tape at one o'clock.

A limo whisked Julia to the station just after noon, and a bevy of assistants led her to the makeup room, where an excitable young man managed to flatter and criticize in one breath.

"You really have lovely features," he told her. "If I had more time I could do fantastic things with your eyes. Add a little shadow . . ." His brush moved rapidly over her lids. "And look at those cheekbones. A little color . . ." He dipped another brush into a pot of powder, and when he finished, Julia opened one eye and peeked. The face that looked back at her reminded her of someone she knew, but certainly not of Julia Shelton.

He whisked off her cape. "You have great potential, if only there was more time."

"Well, there's not," Tiffany said from the door. "She's due on the set. Polly's here and anxious to meet you," she told Julia as she led her down the hall. "We're taping your segment first. Did you get lots of rest?"

"Oh, lots," Julia lied.

"Great, because Polly's still a little hoarse. You may have to do most of the talking, but it's only fifteen minutes."

"Only fifteen," Julia groaned.

"Cheer up," Tiffany said encouragingly. "And remember, you got a phone call in the Polo Lounge."

"So I must be a star," Julia said.

"Exactly." Tiffany led her down another hall, through Door 1-A, dodging the lights, stepping over cables coiled like giant snakes along the floor, and gave her a little push. "Here she is, Polly," she said proudly. "Dr. Julia Shelton."

Polly Anderson didn't look so fierce, after all, Julia decided. Tall and slender, with deep brown eyes and laugh lines she'd taken no special pains to hide—which, Julia suspected, gave the makeup man a fit—she could have been anyone's favorite aunt. Julia looked quickly over her shoulder and saw Tiffany flash a smile. Maybe it wouldn't be so difficult, after all.

"Dr. Shelton," Polly said, extending her hand. "I'm going to begin by calling you Julia, if I may."

"Certainly," Julia replied.

"I'm Polly. We've invited some environmental groups to join us in the audience. They'll be especially supportive." Her voice was low and husky and just as friendly as her face.

What wasn't so friendly was the trio of cameras trained on Julia and the rows of seats that seemed to go on forever, empty at the moment, but still intimidating.

Polly seemed to understand her helplessness. "Don't worry," she said, leading Julia to a sofa in the middle of the stage. "Pretend we're at home and you're talking just to me."

Julia nodded. It sounded like a good idea, but the reality was not so homey, especially when the audience began to file in like a great, intimidating beast, breathing, shuffling, moving all the time. The lights went on and blinded her for a moment. At least they kept her from seeing faces in the audience.

Taping time drew closer. Julia's heart began to thump alarmingly, and she felt her cheeks grow hot. She told herself that she was a grown woman, head of an important project.

It didn't help. Julia knew she was panicking. Would she be able to think of anything to say? She clutched the photographs of the wolves she'd brought, hoping to find some solace in the warm, golden eyes of Taza and Cochise, but someone was already setting up an easel for the pictures, then someone else was prying them out of her clutches.

"Two minutes, Polly," a disembodied voice called.

Polly settled beside Julia on the sofa, looked over her notes quickly and put them aside. "This is going to be fun," she told Julia. "Don't worry, you won't run out of things to say."

How had Polly known that was her worry? Julia asked herself.

Then the voice called out again, "One minute." With a flurry Tiffany rushed onto the set and thrust a note into Julia's hand.

"He was really insistent," she said. "I was afraid he would come right up here onstage if I didn't bring the note to you."

She hurried off, and Julia opened the folded paper.

You have a date after the show with your number-
one fan. Love, Jake.

Julia looked at the audience but saw nothing beyond
the blinding lights. It didn't matter. He was here.

And that made everything easy.

Once she started talking, she found it difficult to stop.
She knew that would amuse Jake. She could imagine
the twinkle in his eye when she explained how her life-
long interest in animals and fascination with wolves
had led to her fight to start the project, which had led
to her search for funding and then to other groups that
had won their battles. She really got going on that, but
the audience seemed interested and so, happily, did
Polly.

"Other projects have a head start on us," Julia explained. "The gray wolves in the Western states and the
red wolf in North Carolina were returned to their hab-
itats several years ago. Our experiment is the first with
the Mexican brown wolf, and if we're not successful,
I'm afraid they'll be doomed to extinction."

The audience really picked that up, and as the cameras focused on the photos of her wolves, Julia talked
about each one, their different personalities and habits
that made them as interesting and likable as domestic
animals.

She was surprised when she felt Polly's hand on her
arm, their prearranged signal that time was up.

"This has been a fascinating interview," Polly said,
"and you truly are a remarkable woman, Julia. We're

going to put the name and phone number of your organization on the screen, so our audience at home and in the studio can find out more about the project. I realize donations are needed, and I'm going to start the ball rolling with a thousand-dollar check to adopt that beautiful Nokomis."

Julia's thanks were lost in a round of applause. Miraculously, it was all over. The tape stopped rolling; the cameras were moved to set up new angles, and Polly was on her feet, greeting the next guest.

Tiffany showed up to lead Julia off the stage. "You were as great as Beth said you'd be," she said, bubbling with enthusiasm, "and Polly is really pleased, I can tell. The response is going to be overwhelming. Be prepared," she warned.

But Julia was vibrant, waiting, looking over Tiffany's shoulder. And then she saw him, tall and handsome, smiling at her, his arms open. She stepped forward and he held her close.

"THE FIRST THING I want to do," Julia said to Jake, "is get this gunk off my face."

"You look gorgeous, gunk and all," he said, kissing her thoroughly.

They were in the back of the station's limo, oblivious to the driver, who didn't seem interested, anyway, as he maneuvered through traffic toward the hotel.

"What made you change your mind?" she asked between his kisses. "About coming to L.A.?"

"Lots of things," he equivocated.

"Such as?" She wanted to know.

"Such as, you needed me."

"You don't know how much," she said fervently.

"I didn't know at first," he said, "but now I believe I do. By the way, you were terrific."

"All because you were there. Thanks, Jake."

As soon as they got to the room, true to her word, Julia headed straight for the bath, opened a jar of cleansing cream and applied a huge glop to her face. "So long, show biz," she said.

She emerged from the bathroom, face shining, cheeks rosy, where she'd scrubbed off the last traces of blush, to hear the pop of a cork.

"Just delivered," he said. "From Polly and Tiffany." He poured Julia a glass of champagne and handed it to her, and reached for another glass.

For a moment Julia panicked. Was Jake throwing away his hard-earned sobriety to celebrate with her— or had the few hours he'd spent in L.A. changed him completely? Then she saw the mineral water bottle beside the champagne and breathed a sigh of relief.

"Don't worry," he said, filling his glass with mineral water.

"I wasn't," she lied.

"Yes, you were."

"All right, but I can't help thinking about what you said. L.A.'s a dangerous place for you to be."

"Not when we're here together. And we're going to be here until tomorrow. It's all arranged."

"Jake, I'm so glad, but . . ."

"What, Julia?"

"Are you sure?" she asked, looking at him over the rim of her glass.

"I'm sure." He clinked his glass against hers. "After all, I'm the kind of guy who'd do anything for the gal he loves."

Julia put down her glass carefully, so she wouldn't break the spell. "What did you say?" she asked softly.

"I said, I'm the kind of guy..."

"No, the last part."

"Oh, you mean that stuff about love?"

Julia nodded.

"It went something like this—I love you, Julia."

She looked at him, eyes wide and filling with tears. Then she threw herself into his arms. "I love you, too, Jake, more than you can know. Oh, I love you, I love you."

They fell together onto the bed, laughing, touching each other with eager hands. He cupped her breast and whispered softly into her ear. "I not only love you, I want to make love to you."

"In the middle of the afternoon?"

"What better time," he inquired, his fingers reaching for the buttons on her blouse, "than the afternoon?" He pulled her blouse off carefully. "What better time," he repeated, "than the afternoon, with hours stretching before us? We'll need them, Julia, because I plan to love every inch of you."

And he did, fiercely, eagerly, thoroughly, as if they'd been apart for weeks instead of days. Hours later they lay together on the rumpled bed, their bodies still damp in the afterglow of passion, the sunlight that had filtered through the curtains beginning to fade.

"It's getting dark," Julia said, raising herself on one elbow and looking down at Jake. She pushed a lock of damp hair from his face and couldn't resist kissing him. "We've wasted the whole afternoon."

"Wasted?"

She laughed. "And *what* a waste!"

"I'll say. But L.A.'s open all night. There's plenty of time."

"Good," she murmured, "because I'm having too much fun to move now." After a moment she added, "We can stay in tonight. Call room service and order some terribly decadent meal."

"Still worried about me?"

"A little."

He touched her cheek. "Thanks, Doc, but it's okay. You're with me."

"I know, but still, you don't have to take the chance."

"I don't have to, but I need to. I need to face the past, what I used to be. Before I didn't want to, I hid from it. But I was alone then." He took her lovingly into his arms. "But I'm not alone anymore. We'll see the city together."

9

"JAKE," Julia murmured, "we ought to get up...."

"Roll out of bed?"

"Hmm," she said.

"Soon." They were still lying entangled in each other's arms, but he managed to pull her even closer. She snuggled against his body.

"It's late," she reminded him.

"In Pierson County, maybe. In L.A. the night's still young." He stretched.

"Which is exactly why we should get up."

"So you do want to go to the clubs?"

"Yes," she admitted. "Now that you're here, I want to see what L.A.'s nightlife is like."

"There's a lot I want to show you," he said.

Neither of them seemed inclined to leave the warmth of their bed, Julia reflected.

"Then why aren't we going?" he inquired.

"Can't imagine," she replied.

"I'll make the first move." He turned on the bedside light.

It bathed them in a rosy-pink glow and prompted Julia to reach up and touch Jake's face. "Thanks," she said.

"For?"

"For coming here to be with me."

"I told you before, anything for the woman I love. And I do love you, Julia." He sealed his declaration with a kiss.

She forgot all about dinner and their night on the town, settling comfortably against his shoulder and asking, "When did you know? For sure?"

"The first time I saw you."

"Oh, no, Jake Forrester. You can't get away with that."

"You don't believe me?" He kissed her again, though it didn't help his case.

"Not for a moment," she said. "You wanted me then. You told me that. But I'm talking about love, l-o-v-e. And I'd appreciate a romantic answer."

"Well," he drawled, "let's see." He closed his eyes and pretended to think deep thoughts. "Maybe it was when you told me off."

"Which time?" she teased.

Jake laughed. "There were so many, it's hard to say. Oh, I know, that day you walked into my office with your dander up."

"No, Jake, you were only flirting then."

"So were you," he reminded her.

"I was not," she countered, then remembered that she'd been trying to get him to drive her home. "At least, I didn't know it at the time."

He gave her a hug. "Liar. Anyway, I think it was that night out on the desert, or maybe at the barbecue, or maybe..."

"Jake." She put her fingers upon his lips. "You don't even remember."

"No, I don't," he admitted, looking down at her. "I can't imagine a time when I didn't love you, so how can I possibly remember when it first happened?"

"Oh, Jake." Julia was touched.

"It seems like I've always loved you," he murmured.

She fell quiet; tears were building.

"Hey," he asked gently, "isn't that a good enough answer?"

She looked at him, blinking. "That's about the best answer in the world, Jake Forrester."

"Even if I'm not sure when it happened, I know when I first realized it—that I loved you, I mean."

She waited patiently.

"It was when I took your side against Fred."

"Oh?" Julia recalled that earlier conversation very well. "But you said that had nothing to do with me, that you were just doing your job."

"As it happened, what I wanted and what my job demanded were one and the same."

"Lucky you," she said jokingly.

But Jake wasn't joking. "It wouldn't have mattered. My heart was on your side. Fred couldn't have done anything to change that."

Julia had wondered about that, though she hadn't wanted to confront him. Now she knew, and her last doubts disappeared.

"Time to get up," Jake proposed. "We've got places to go and things to do."

They showered together quickly.

"Can I go out like this, with my hair still wet?" Julia asked.

"It's the style in L.A.," he told her.

"Wet hair?"

"Sure." He wrapped her in a towel, dried her quickly and pulled her naked body close. "Now," he said, hands exploring anew, "what was all that nonsense about going out?"

"We *are*," she said, pulling the towel back into place. "You promised."

"What about . . ." He reached for the towel again.

She pushed his hand away. "Later," she replied. "There's a time and place for everything."

"Speaking of that," Jake said as he released her, "you haven't told me when *you* fell in love with me."

Julia wandered into the bedroom, toweling her hair.

"It had to have been love at first sight," he quipped, rummaging through his suitcase for underwear.

"Wrong," she shot back.

"You mean you weren't carried away when I strode out of the desert and into your life?"

"Frankly I thought you were rude, macho, conceited—"

"Wait, enough." He held up her hand.

"And just a little bit devious," she concluded.

"Some of my better traits," he bantered.

Julia pulled her red dress out of the closet. "I hope you don't mind the repetition, but when it comes to dressy, this is it. I wore this for the interview."

"It's the dress you were wearing when I first fell in love with you," he said, dodging when she took a swing at him.

"Now who's the liar?"

"You'll never know," he teased. "Tell me, Julia, when did it happen for you?"

Julia slipped into the dress. "When I learned that you could be kind and loyal and loving. As well as very, very sexy," she added.

Jake had pulled on a pair of pants and a striped shirt he left open at the neck. Julia hadn't seen him dressed this way before, and her heart skipped a beat. He looked different, sophisticated.

"Yes, very sexy," she repeated, remembering. "I think I started falling in love the first night we went to bed."

Jake had tucked in his shirt and was buckling his belt. He stopped and reached for her. "We didn't just go to bed, Julia," he said seriously. "We made love."

"I know that." Now they were both serious. "I feel so lucky," she said. "In fact, I'm almost afraid to say how happy I am, for fear it'll all get taken away."

"No one can take this from us." He held her close and ran his hands through her still-damp hair. "You know, we're more alike than anyone realizes. Both of us are loners. We'd shut off our feelings and pushed them aside. Yet when we made love it was like a door opening. Now we're afraid of what we might lose. But we can't lose it, we won't lose it, I promise. Do you believe me, Julia?"

She nodded, her head against his chest.

"Together we can face anything and come out on top."

Julia put her arms around him, breathing in the fresh, clean smell of his shirt. The fine cotton was soft against her cheek. "I believe in us, Jake."

The words surprised her. For so long she had believed only in herself, trusted only herself. Now here she was, putting her faith in Jake Forrester, too.

"I'll never let you down," he answered. "And that's a promise."

"You don't have to make promises."

"Oh, yes, I do. And commitments. I was thinking about the night of the barbecue, when you made me so damned angry talking about commitments—"

"I never did," she said defensively.

"Maybe not. Maybe it was so much on my mind, I figured it had to be on yours. I was falling in love then," he told her tenderly. "You were beginning to change my life then."

"I hope for the better."

"You know it," he said, giving her a little push. "Now finish dressing and let's get out of here, before I drag you back to bed."

JAKE HAD RENTED A CAR, and as the valet drove it up to the door of the hotel, Jake stepped forward to meet him. Suddenly Julia saw the man who'd once been a part of this town, suave, handsome, in charge, dressed with a casual elegance, one hand brushing back a strand of hair as he reached into his pocket with the other for a tip.

The car was a low-slung red Alfa Romeo, so different from the four-wheel drive. *Which was his real life?* The question plagued her throughout the evening, although she mentioned nothing to Jake.

They turned out of the driveway and started down Sunset Boulevard. Julia was nervous. Jake was going out to confront his past. What would happen when he was faced with the life he'd fled from years before? This glorious night could end not so gloriously.

She didn't want that. Maybe there was a way to prevent it. "Jake," she said softly, "why don't we go to someplace different, someplace you haven't been before? Something Italian," she suggested. "I'd love Italian."

Maybe, just maybe, that would take him away from the old haunts.

He glanced at her with a smile. "Just what I had in mind, but not *any* Italian restaurant. The best one. I was a regular there," he said, focusing on the brightly lit boulevard. "I wonder if they'll remember me?"

Julia's heart sank. Jake was going to be surrounded by all his old temptations—including alcohol. "Actually, it doesn't have to be Italian...."

"Don't worry. It'll be all right. I'm not going to drink. I know you love taking care of people, but I also know what I'm doing. Trust me."

Trust me. That wasn't so easy. It had always been difficult for Julia to trust anyone. Yet she had depended on him before, and he hadn't let her down. Now, against all odds, she had to learn to trust him. Maybe because she loved him.

As they drove through Hollywood, Julia relaxed and watched the people strolling along Sunset Boulevard—transvestites, hustlers, teenagers.

Then Jake headed toward Beverly Hills and the scene changed dramatically. Here, there were very few people walking. Instead, the streets were clogged with Jaguar and BMW convertibles, stretch limos and Rolls-Royce sedans.

"Where are they headed?" she asked.

"To the chic restaurants and clubs," he replied.

Jake turned onto a side street and pulled up in front of a building with a brick facade and a dark green awning. "Is this a restaurant?" she asked. There was no sign outside.

"The best one in town." A valet appeared, as if from nowhere.

"How do people even know it's here?" Julia asked as a doorman appeared and ushered them in.

Jake took her hand and led her inside. "They don't, which is exactly the way Arturo wants it."

"We aren't people?"

"Nope. We're special people. At least for tonight."

"Have you a reservation?" the maître d' asked as they approached.

"No, we don't," Jake told him.

"Well, I'm afraid we have nothing available."

Jake's expression didn't change, and his voice remained low and easy. "There always used to be a table for me at Arturo's, no matter what the crowd."

Julia couldn't tell if he expected or even wanted to be recognized. It was simply a test, something he had to do.

"Or maybe you just don't recognize me, Gregory," he added.

Gregory looked up from the table plan on his desk. He was a tall, thin man, balding, a few strips of hair combed back across the shiny dome of his head. He looked tired, as if the weight of the world rested on his narrow shoulders. Running one of the city's best restaurants must take its toll, Julia decided.

He peered at Jake over the rims of his half glasses, then a smile of recognition lit up his face. "Mr. Forrester." He reached out and pumped Jake's hand. "I thought you were dead," he declared.

Julia shuddered, but the remark didn't seem to faze her companion.

"Came pretty close," he admitted, "but with the help of friends I survived."

"Well, you did live a dangerous life."

"That's all over now, Gregory. Tonight we're here to enjoy a long, leisurely meal, just like ordinary people."

"Well, not quite, Mr. Forrester. Ordinary people don't dine at Arturo's," Gregory corrected.

"You're absolutely right. I've just been explaining that to Ms. Shelton."

"We'll let the lady see for herself, shall we?" Gregory suggested, glancing at his chart. "I see that a table has just become available." He looked up, his long, sad face suddenly transformed by his grin.

"That's remarkable," Jake deadpanned.

"It happens at the oddest times," Gregory agreed. "Like magic."

"What about the old crowd?" Jake asked him. "Any of them ever show up?"

"They do, they do, occasionally." He raised one hand and a young waiter appeared. "Dave, table number three for Mr. Forrester and his guest," Gregory commanded. And then to Jake he said, "I'll keep my eye out for anyone special."

Dave had obviously concluded from Gregory's behavior that this couple was among the special guests, and he treated them accordingly, being just solicitous enough to please, without becoming obsequious.

Jake waved away the menu and asked about the specials. With Dave's help he narrowed down the selection to angel hair pasta with Arturo sauce, scallops on spinach linguine or lobster-filled ravioli. Julia chose the scallops.

"I'll have the same," Jake said. "And we'll begin with an order of fried calamari."

"And for your wine?" the waiter asked.

"Nothing for me," Julia said.

"Nonsense," Jake told her. "This is a special night and it calls for a special wine." He chose one from the list. When the waiter left, Jake commented, "It's absolutely uncivilized to have an Italian meal without a good wine. And I won't see you deprived of that pleasure just because you fell in love with a recovering alcoholic."

"You're right about the love part, anyway," Julia said.

That was the last personal remark she managed for the next hour. As they ate, a steady parade of Jake's friends made their way to the table to greet them, talk about old times with Jake, and ask what he was up to now.

None of them was prepared for the answer, and Julia sat back, amused, as each responded with visible disbelief. Quite a few of them were Jake's former clients. They included a television actor who'd hired him to find his runaway daughter, a writer involved in a financial dispute with his agent, whom he'd suspected of being his wife's lover, and a former police officer, who'd been obsessed with solving a murder that had occurred when he was a rookie.

They weren't all men, either, which didn't surprise Julia in the least.

By the time they'd finished the main course, the interruptions had slowed.

"Sorry," Jake apologized. "I really didn't know so many of them would appear. Like Gregory, I guess I suspected they were dead."

"I enjoyed all the stories," Julia admitted. "But I'm glad to have you to myself again."

He reached out and took her hand.

"Some of the female clients may be watching," she warned.

"Let 'em watch," he said, promptly leaned closer and kissed her thoroughly.

"Jake!" she exclaimed, embarrassed.

"Julia, you have to remember that we're in my town, on my turf, and whatever we do is the right and proper thing to do."

"Just because we're doing it?"

"Exactly," he said, kissing her again.

They lingered over dessert and coffee and were still at the table, talking softly and finishing their cappuccinos, when a heavy, meaty hand fell upon Jake's shoulder.

"I never thought I'd see the day, but you're back, and I'm overjoyed."

"Norm, it's been a long time." Jake stood and shook his hand warmly, then introduced Julia, explaining that Norm Freeman had been one of his most loyal clients.

"Best paying, too," Norm said.

"Well, you must admit, Norm, I put in more man-hours for you than anyone else over the years." He drew up a chair from the next table for the newcomer.

Norm was short and powerfully built, Julia noted. He was wearing a gold chain, a gold watch, and gold rings on two pudgy fingers and exuded an aura of wealth and power. She felt a bit intimidated by him.

"So," Norm said, "it's a relief to see you back here at Arturo's where you belong."

Jake dismissed that remark with a wave of his hand.

"And looking fit, I might add." Norm signaled to a waiter.

"That's because my problems are all behind me."

"Good," Norm said heartily, "because mine are not."
Dave came up to the table. "A brandy for me, and Mr.
Forrester will have the same. And for you, my dear?"
he asked Julia.

She shook her head. "Just coffee, thank you."

"And coffee for me," Jake said.

"That's all?" Norm inquired.

"That's all, my friend. I'm on the wagon for life."

Norm shook his head and told Julia, "Considering
the source, I believe him. Jake's always been straight."

The brandy and coffees arrived. "In fact, this might
just be a blessing in disguise," Norm continued. "Because, old pal, I have a job that is right up your alley at
a salary that will knock you over, and sobriety won't
hurt one bit."

Jake laughed. "I'm not looking for a job, Norm."

"At this price you'll look. It's chief of security. Tai-
lor-made for you."

"So is the job I have now."

"I'll double the pay, whatever it is," Norm said immediately.

Jake leaned over and named a figure he knew was
small by L.A. standards.

"That's all you get? Well, that I'll quadruple," Norm
told him. "Whaddaya do for such a low salary, anyway?"

"I'm sheriff of Pierson County, New Mexico."

The look of disbelief on Norm's face was classic.
"County sheriff? Sorry, my boy, it just won't play. Bad

casting. No, you're a big-city dude, always have been and always will be."

"In the past, Norm."

Norm turned to Julia. "How long have you been in town?" he asked.

"I've been here two days, and Jake just arrived—"

"I see, I see. Not long enough. A couple more days, and you'll begin thinking differently," he told Jake. "Just call me, my boy. You know where I am. Same address, same phone number. Nothing changes." He stood up. "Now I gotta get back to the old lady, but you call me, okay?"

Jake shook Norm's hand. "Thanks for the vote of confidence, but we're heading back home tomorrow."

Julia realized she'd been holding her breath, waiting for his answer. Slowly she breathed again, relieved.

"I'm depressed by that news but not defeated." Norm reached into his pocket and whipped out a card. "I accept calls from all over, so why not New Mexico?" Then with a nod to Julia and another pat of Jake's shoulder, he walked away.

Julia shook her head in wonder.

"Quite a character, huh?" Jake asked.

"A real wheeler-dealer, I imagine."

"Oh, that he is. Owns a TV production company that grinds out some of the top sitcoms. I used to do background checks, research we called it, on his free-lance staff, and I often babysat the less reliable actors, who had a tendency to disappear. He stuck by me a lot longer than some of the others, even when I started going down fast."

"He really likes you," Julia said. "And he seems serious about the job offer."

Jake shrugged and motioned for the check. "Just big-city talk. Everybody loves everybody. . . for the moment." Then he smiled with visible pleasure. "But since it's only for a day, I must admit it's fun to be back—and to be missed."

He fell silent, and Julia wondered what he was thinking.

"So," he said finally, "what's next? Dancing, bar-hopping, or back to the hotel?"

"Back to the hotel," she replied without hesitation.

He nodded. "We have an early flight tomorrow."

Julia sat silent during the drive back to the hotel.

"A penny for your thoughts," Jake said a few minutes later.

"I was thinking about tonight," she said, "about your friends and the life you left behind. It was very different from Pierson County."

"An understatement," Jake told her.

"Different and better?" she asked.

"Different and more glamorous, more exciting. But not better. Besides, it's all in the past, Julia."

"It wouldn't have to be—in the past." She had to face the facts; she couldn't ignore her fears. "Your job in Pierson County could be in jeopardy, Jake, especially after that last episode at my place. If Norm really wants to hire you, well, that could be a perfect solution."

"Fred's not the only registered voter in Pierson County," Jake reminded her.

"You're right. The cattlemen have votes, too."

"Quit worrying about me and Fred, will you?" Jake turned at the light, pulled into a side street and stopped the car. "Seems like I'm always stopping to give you a lecture," he said. "But this is serious. We still have a few hours of vacation together, and we're going to enjoy it without any interference from Fred Gilmer. So if you have anything else to say about him, say it now, and let's get it over with."

"I can't stop thinking about him," Julia admitted, "how you chose me over Fred, how you went against him...."

"I did what I wanted to do, Julia. It also happens that what I wanted was right. Fred knows that. Eventually he'll come to his senses."

"And if he doesn't..."

"He will," Jake said. "I know the man. He's really a decent guy. But if he doesn't come around, well, I'm feeling pretty good about my life now. I can handle it."

Julia wasn't satisfied with Jake's answer. And she had no faith at all in Fred. If things got rough in Pierson County, there was so much waiting for Jake here in L.A. A new job, old friends. He'd conquered his problem with alcohol. What was there to keep him from returning to the big city?

Jake leaned over and kissed her on the forehead. "Now that's enough about Fred. We're supposed to be having fun." He looked at his watch. "Less than ten hours left, so let's fill them with excitement—" he bent and kissed her "—and a little healthy lust."

His kiss was demanding, and Julia responded to him as she always did, completely and with abandon. Still, the comfort she received from his kiss couldn't prevent her from worrying about tomorrow. What would happen next?

10

JAKE PICKED UP THE PHONE on the first ring. He was expecting the call.

"It's time for us to talk, Jake."

"I'm available, Fred."

"I heard you've been in L.A."

"You heard right. Just got back this morning." Jake put his feet up on his desk and leaned back in his office chair, more relaxed than he'd been in a long time. Fred's call didn't faze him.

There was a pause, then Fred asked, "How was the city?"

"Hasn't changed much."

"A good trip, though?" Fred probed.

"Better than I had hoped for or even imagined," Jake said honestly.

"That successful, huh? Does that mean you could be heading back to the Coast, now that you're...uh, rehabilitated?"

Jake laughed. "You can't get rid of me that easily, Fred. Besides, I know you didn't call to discuss my trip to L.A. What's on your mind?"

"We need to talk about the future."

"That's pretty ambiguous. Anybody's future in particular?"

"Yep," Fred replied. "Yours, Jake."

Jake waited without answering.

"Something happened while you were gone. Let's just say how you decide to handle the situation will affect all of us."

"Could you be a little more specific?"

"When you get here, Jake. I'm waiting."

JULIA WAS AT THE COMPUTER, trying to concentrate on the blips in spite of her weariness. She wondered how Jake was doing. Fresh and bright-eyed after a big breakfast and several cups of coffee on the flight, he'd gone straight to his office when they got back from L.A. Determined to keep up with him, Julia had headed for the ranch and gotten in touch with Rafe on the two-way radio.

She'd found the wolves' new habitat on the computer. Then Rafe moved out of radio range into the field, and his voice had faded away.

She had tried to follow the pack's movements on her own, but her eyes kept closing. No wonder, Julia told herself. They'd gotten hardly any sleep last night after returning from the restaurant, dozing, making love, dozing again. When it was time to leave, they'd climbed aboard the airport bus and managed to catch a few more winks.

"Julia!"

She went to the front door where Beth was banging. "Why did you lock me out?"

Julia opened the door, laughing. "Frankly, I forgot you were working today."

Beth came in and headed straight for the stove. "Are you planning to stay up or go to bed?"

"Stay up," Julia said.

"In that case I'm making a pot of coffee, Julia, because you're half-asleep right now."

Julia sank into a chair at the kitchen table. "I know, but I wanted to follow the wolves and see the new habitat on the screen."

"Wait till tomorrow," Beth suggested, "and you can go out with Rafe to see the real thing."

"You're right." Julia accepted the coffee and took a sip. "This may do the trick."

Beth settled beside Julia and asked, "How'd it go?"

Julia gestured vaguely. "So-so."

"You can't fool me," Beth replied. "I talked to Tiffany last night, and she said you were a huge success." Beth glanced at her watch. "It's airing today—in a couple of hours. We'll have to watch."

"I'm not sure I can last that long."

"I'll tape it," Beth promised. "Now, other than the show, how did you like L.A.?"

"It's a nice place to visit, but..."

"You wouldn't want to live there," Beth finished. "But I bet Jake was glad to see L.A. again. Did you two live it up?"

"Not exactly," Julia said. She was still plagued by thoughts of how comfortable he'd seemed there, how well he'd fitted in. Not only were many of his friends there, but Norm had a job waiting for him, as well.

Beth was already off on another tangent. "Jake looks great. He seems to have recovered quicker than you."

"When did you see him?"

"Just a little while ago. He and Dad were going off someplace for a meeting."

"Why?" Julia asked.

"To talk about the future."

"How do you know?" Julia was concerned by the news.

"That's what Dad said." Beth poured her another cup of coffee. "What's the matter, Julia?" she asked. "Are you worried about what they were discussing?"

"No," Julia lied.

"It's going to be all right," Beth said uncertainly, clearly trying to convince them both. "Dad isn't going to threaten Jake, if that's what you think. He's safe, Julia."

Whatever Beth thought, Julia knew something else about Jake. He was being wooed by L.A., and she couldn't fight off a feeling of foreboding.

"There's something you don't know," she told Beth. "Jake loved being in L.A., and they rolled out the red carpet for him. He even got a job offer. If he and Fred can't solve their problems, I think Jake could walk away from here."

"Don't be silly, Julia," Beth retorted. "You're the most important thing in his life. He's not going to leave you and go back to L.A."

Julia didn't answer; she just hoped Beth was right. But what if she was wrong?

IT WAS TWO O'CLOCK. Julia had woken up from a nap, Beth had gone through all the mail, and it was almost time for *Anderson in the a.m.* to air.

The phone rang. "I'll get it," Julia said, wide-awake and feeling clearheaded. She expected it would be Rafe, calling about the wolves' status, or Jake, regarding his conversation with Fred.

She listened in silence and when she hung up, chose her words carefully. "Beth, there's been an accident. It's all right," she continued before the younger woman had a chance to respond. "Your father overturned his Jeep. Rafe was driving back on the old trail and saw the accident...."

"Julia—"

"Your dad was thrown out, and his leg's broken. Rafe took him to the hospital."

Beth grabbed her purse and headed for the door.

"I'm coming with you," Julia said. "I'll drive."

"Yes, yes," Beth agreed. "Does he have any other injuries?"

"They aren't sure," Julia said as they climbed into the car. "Maybe some internal injuries, but his vital signs look good. He'll be fine, Beth."

RAFE MET THEM in the Pierson County Hospital waiting room. Beth clung to him, and he did his best to reassure her.

"Don't worry, honey," he said. "He's in Recovery now. They'll let us know as soon as we can see him."

"Should I call the ranch and tell them?" Beth asked.

"I think that's a good idea," Julia said.

"How is he, really?" she asked Rafe when Beth left in search of a pay phone.

"He'll make it," Rafe said. "He's a tough old bastard. I have to admit that for a second there, when I saw him lying in the dirt, I considered driving on by."

"You didn't," Julia said.

"Only for a moment. Especially when I thought if it had been me on the ground, Fred wouldn't have stopped."

"You don't really believe that."

"I'm not sure whether I do or not, but I couldn't leave him. And besides, he's Beth's father."

"I think he's a good man, deep down," Julia said, trying to sound convincing.

"Won't he have a fit when he comes out of surgery and finds my blood in his veins?"

"You gave him a transfusion?" Julia asked.

"Yep. Does that make us blood brothers?"

Julia smiled. "He'll be grateful that his blood type and yours match. Here comes Beth."

"They'll be standing by at the ranch," Beth reported. "I doubt if much work will get done, though. The men are so loyal...." She looked at Rafe. "I had trouble tracking Jake down, though," she said. "I tried his home and his office. No answer."

"Maybe we should have him paged," Julia suggested.

"That's not really necessary, Julia," Rafe said. "He's just out and about on business. No point in bothering him until we have a report from the doctors."

Julia nodded, but she was worried about Jake. What had happened after his meeting with Fred? "Why don't you two go over to the cafeteria and get something to eat?" she suggested. "Rafe's probably famished, and this might turn out to be a long day."

"Do you think it'll be all right for us to leave for a little while?" Beth asked.

"Of course," Julia said. "I'll be here, and I'll come and get you if anything happens."

Beth agreed grudgingly, asking Rafe, "He will be okay, won't he?"

Rafe slipped an arm around her waist. "He's a tough old bird, honey. You know that. He'll be around for a long time, now that he has Santana blood in him."

Julia waited until they had left, then walked down the hall to the coffee machine. But the coffee was terrible and did nothing to keep her mind off Jake. Where the hell was he, and had something happened before Gilmer's Jeep rolled?

Clutching her cup, Julia eased into a chair and looked at her watch. It was four o'clock. The day was only half-over, but between the early-morning flight from L.A., the race across the desert to the hospital and this interminable wait for word from the doctors, it seemed like midnight.

She was considering trying to call Jake again when Rafe and Beth returned from the cafeteria, and the doctors, masks and stethoscopes dangling around their necks, stepped into the waiting room.

"Is he all right, is Daddy all right?" Beth asked, rushing toward them. "Can I see him?"

"He came through the surgery with flying colors," one doctor said. "He's just getting out of Recovery."

"When can we see him?" Beth wanted to know.

"They're bringing him out now to Room—" the doctor checked his chart, "—twenty-three."

Beth rushed down the hall toward the room.

The doctors made no move to leave. "There's some internal injury," one of them said, "but we've stopped the bleeding and repaired the damage to his spleen. His leg was badly broken, and the healing process will be prolonged, but in time everything should be back to normal."

Julia didn't quite know how to respond. The doctors were treating her and Rafe as if they were Fred's family.

Rafe took over, nodding and shaking the doctors' hands before heading down the hall. Julia shrugged and followed.

"Wait in the hall!" a nurse called after them. "No more than one visitor at a time."

Rafe and Julia waited obediently until Beth came out and walked into Rafe's arms. "He's going to be all right," she said, clearly relieved, "and you saved him, Rafe!"

"No, Beth, I—"

"You did! You saved him out on the desert and again when you gave blood, and I told him so."

Rafe looked at Julia over Beth's head, visibly uncomfortable.

"He wants to see you and Julia," Beth told them.

"Beth—"

"You'd better hurry," she added. "He's getting groggy."

"Maybe we should postpone . . ." Julia began.

"No, no," Beth insisted. "He's adamant. Now, go on in." She pushed them toward the door.

The nurse who'd cautioned them to visit one at a time had disappeared, so they went into the room.

Fred seemed much smaller lying down than he ever had standing or mounted on a horse, Julia thought. He had a plaster cast on his leg and he was swathed in bandages, but his face, though pale, appeared tranquil in repose. His eyes were heavy-lidded, and when he spoke his voice was hoarse.

"I didn't call you in here to thank you, although I suppose I should," he said to Rafe.

Julia bit back a smile. A brush with death hadn't stopped Fred's brusqueness.

"No thanks necessary, sir," Rafe said.

"As usual, you're off the mark, Santana," Fred said. "You saved my life twice, I understand. Once in the desert and once in the operating room."

"Well, I—"

"Don't quibble," Fred advised. "We'll talk about it . . . later." His voice faded. He *was* tired, Julia realized, but still in charge.

"Yes, sir," Rafe said almost meekly. He was trying to do the best he could for Beth's sake, and he was doing an outstanding job, Julia thought.

Fred waved a weak hand, then took a deep and obviously painful breath. "Now, something more urgent . . ."

Rafe leaned forward.

"Urgent," Fred repeated.

"I think the sedative is taking effect," Julia whispered.

"Jake . . ."

Julia moved closer to the bed. "What about Jake?" she asked. "Is he in some kind of danger?"

"Yes," Fred repeated, "danger."

"Fred, tell me . . ." Julia urged.

Fred's lips moved, but no words were forthcoming.

"Where's Jake?" Julia gripped Fred's hand, willing him to stay awake, to talk to her.

"Take it easy, Julia," Rafe advised.

"But he's fading, Rafe. He's going to sleep."

"No," Fred murmured. "Not yet. Have to tell . . . ."

Julia's feelings of foreboding returned. Something was wrong. Jake was in trouble, and Fred Gilmer, the one man who could tell her what was going on, was drifting into a drugged sleep.

Then he slowly opened his eyes again. "Told Jake this morning . . ."

Julia could feel him struggle to stay awake and focused.

"Men, tracking wolves..."

"Yes?" Julia prompted.

"Rumors about the big one..."

"Cochise." Julia tightened her grip on Fred's arm. "Are they after Cochise?"

Rafe took over. "It doesn't matter which wolf," he told Julia. Then he leaned toward Fred once more. "We need to know where they are. Can you tell us, sir? Where are they?"

"Please," Julia begged, "please."

Fred closed his eyes again, and she prayed he hadn't fallen asleep.

"Wait, Julia," Rafe said. Fred's lips moved slightly, and they strained to hear the words.

"Jake was tracking... El Diablo rocks..."

Julia glanced at Rafe, who nodded as Fred continued to speak. "I came back... to tell."

Then his eyes closed, his breathing grew deep and even, and they knew he'd be asleep for hours.

"Thank you," she whispered. "Thank you, Fred Gilmer." Turning to Rafe she asked urgently, "Do you know the Diablo rocks?"

"Like the palm of my hand. They're just west of the new habitat. Come on, Julia, let's roll."

They filled Beth in as they raced down the hall together. Now that her father was out of danger she wanted to come with them, but Julia shook her head.

"No, there's something more important for you to do, Beth. Jake and Rafe and I can't hold off a bunch of ranchers alone. Find help for us, and send it out to El Diablo."

"What help, Julia? Who?"

"I don't know," Julia said. "You're the PR expert. Organize something."

"I don't have enough time!" Beth cried.

"Get Mom to help," Rafe said. "Call the church, call the school."

"Yes," Beth agreed, obviously formulating a plan. "We'll get a bus, fill it with—"

Julia and Rafe left her at the doors and ran across the parking lot. By the time they'd climbed into the truck, Julia's thoughts were on Jake.

"THERE IT IS!" shouted Rafe over the roar of the engine, "El Diablo! The Devil!"

Julia could make out the twin peaks of a rocky formation, two jagged points that looked very much like the horns of the devil.

Then Rafe swung the truck to the west, approaching one of the large outcroppings. "If they're at the pass, we'll see them before they see us," he told Julia.

He put the truck into low gear and made his way over the bumpy terrain, hugging the wall of rock.

"We're getting close to the pass," he added.

"Are we going through?"

"No way," Rafe said. "Too dangerous, and we don't know where the men are. We'll stay near the rocks. So we can—" He slammed on the brakes, and Julia saw the horsemen, at least a dozen of them, gathered at the mouth of the pass far ahead.

"They're not going through, either. Jake's up there on the rocks, I'm sure of it." Rafe pulled up at a recess in the rocks. "We'll continue on foot," he said. "That way they won't see us until we want them to."

"I don't think we *ever* want them to."

"Eventually they'll have to know we're here, Julia."

They got out and carefully made their way toward the pass, staying close to the rocks. A shot rang out above them. Julia almost screamed. She felt as if she would soon explode.

"It's Jake." Rafe stepped back and scanned the rocks above. "There he is," he said, pointing.

She saw Jake on a precipice above them, facing the men in the pass. He held a rifle in his hands. "Do they see him?" Julia asked.

"I'm not sure they do, but if not, he'll make himself known."

At that moment, Jake stepped into the open. "No one is coming through this pass!" he shouted, clearly aiming directly for the leader of the riders. "That includes you, Buddy Silver. That was just a warning shot. I want all of you out of here, and I want you out now."

"Back down, Forrester!" one of the men shouted back. "We've got you outnumbered and we're coming through!"

"He's trying to head off the whole bunch of them!" Julia gasped.

"That's not as hard as you'd think," Rafe said. "The pass is the only way in, and—"

"They could shoot him!" Julia cried. "We have to stop this!"

"Julia, no!" Despite Rafe's warning she began to scramble up the rocks toward Jake. She could hear Rafe climbing behind her.

The ranchers apparently saw her immediately and began calling out angrily.

"We're after your wolves, lady, and this time nothing's gonna stop us."

"Not you or your boyfriend."

She heard the voice of Buddy Silver. "Talk some sense into the sheriff, lady. If you know what's good for the both of you and those wolves."

When Julia reached Jake's side, he pulled her down roughly behind a sheltering rock. "What the hell are you doing here? This is dangerous, Julia," he said, furious. "There're real bullets in those guns."

"Did you think I wouldn't come?" she asked.

Jake shook his head in wonder and put his arm around her. "Now we're all in it," he said as Rafe slid in beside them.

"Fred never made it back to town for help," Rafe said.

"What happened?" Jake asked, still keeping a careful eye on the men gathered below.

"Hit a rut in the dirt and turned over. I found him and took him to the hospital. That's where we learned that the men were after the wolves again."

"Yeah, someone—probably Silver—started a rumor that Cochise had killed another calf," Jake said. "Then Silver tried to take over when Fred began to back away from the issue."

"What changed Fred's mind?" Rafe asked.

"Julia and Beth, I think, and the attitude of the community. You can't fight public opinion forever."

"And you, Jake," Julia added. "You stood up for what was right."

There was more shouting from the pass.

"Yeah, and what does that get us?" Rafe asked. "We're hiding behind rocks in the blazing sun, and I don't even have a rifle."

Jake moved back into position against the rocks, watching the activity below.

"Beth is sending help," Rafe told him. "Maybe we can hold these guys off until then."

Julia was more worried about the wolves. They'd chosen their hiding place well, protected among the rocks on the other side of the pass, but she knew they'd be frightened by the sound of shots and the smell of men and horses. She didn't know how long this lull would last, and couldn't take a chance on losing the wolves— or bringing harm to Jake and Rafe. "This has got to stop," she said.

Jake made a grab for her, but she'd already slipped out of his grasp and stepped from behind the protective boulder.

"I want to talk to you, Mr. Silver!" she shouted, forgetting she hated confrontation, not even knowing where her courage came from. This was just something she had to do—for the sake of all of them.

"Nothing to talk about, lady!" Silver yelled back. "Except getting those damn wolves outta here before they kill again. Specially that big male."

"Cochise hasn't killed! That's just a rumor!"

Jake and Rafe were suddenly standing beside her.

"I met with Gilmer this morning," Jake added. "He told me the wolves hadn't killed his calf. He made a mistake about that."

Voices rose below in audible disbelief. Then someone called out to challenge the claim. "Why should we believe that?"

"Because it's true!" Rafe yelled angrily.

Jake remained calm. "Gilmer's problems really weren't with the project. They were of a ... a more personal nature. I believe he's worked them out now."

"Yeah, then where the hell is he?"

"In the hospital," Julia answered.

That appeared to cause another stir through the ranks.

"If he were here now—" Julia began again.

"Well, he's not here," Silver said, "and we're coming through that pass, Sheriff. So you and the lady and the Mex just step aside."

Jake raised his rifle, and Julia saw Silver do the same.

"No!" she cried.

"Then let us at the wolves!" Silver demanded. "Or the shooting's gonna start for sure."

Julia knew if that happened they couldn't win. She was sure Jake knew it, too; he gave Rafe and herself a push. Turning, she saw him duck behind a rock, his rifle still ready.

Her mind raced after a solution. Jake had put his career on the line for her not once, but twice, and now he was putting his life in danger. She couldn't let that happen.

"Get down, both of you," Jake commanded. "I'll hold them off."

But Julia had made up her mind. "You win," she called to the men. "I'll close down the project." She stood up again, quite sure of herself this time. "Give me time to recapture the wolves and take them back to captivity. That's all I ask," she went on.

"Julia!" Rafe sounded incredulous.

Jake grabbed her arm. "What the hell are you saying? You can't do this after all you've been through."

"I love the wolves," she said fiercely, shaking him off, "but I love you more, and I want you safe. You've done enough, Jake."

"Like I said, Doc, anything for the woman I love."

Julia looked up at him, not knowing whether to laugh or cry. This was the best moment of her life—and the worst. Jake had proven his love for her. She'd never doubt him again.

"I don't want you to back down," he said.

Julia knew that if she didn't, she might lose the wolves forever. Suddenly that wasn't what mattered most. "I can also do anything for the man I love. I can close down the project, and I will."

Rafe, who'd been standing behind them, suddenly whispered, "Hey, all this self-sacrifice may not be necessary! Beth and the cavalry have arrived."

Plumes of dust rose across the desert. Rafe raised his binoculars.

"The men from Fred's ranch?" Julia asked hopefully, yet dreading another confrontation.

"Look," Rafe said, handing her the binoculars.

"Oh, my heavens," Julia breathed as the caravan came into view.

There were two cars in the vanguard; one bore the TV station logo while the other was from the newspaper. Behind them was a bus from the church.

Julia handed the binoculars to Jake, but he already seemed to have figured it out.

They watched the vehicles unload near the bunched horsemen. Adults got out of vehicles and children began climbing out of the bus.

Julia recognized Beth's blond head below, then Pilar's stout form; she was organizing the children. They had brought the media and the Pierson City children who'd sponsored Cochise.

"They're crazy," Julia said, taking Jake's hand in hers, "and wonderful." They made their way down from the rocks.

Rafe ran toward the crowd. The group of children marched across the desert toward the men, carrying hastily made banners bearing the legend Save Cochise. The men began to curse and then began laughing sheepishly at the ridiculous situation. They put away their rifles. Some recognized their own sons and daughters, slid off their horses and walked forward to meet them. Children broke away from the group and ran to their fathers. Horses whinnied, voices rose, chaos reigned.

Rafe was hugging his mother and Beth when Julia and Jake reached them.

"I wasn't sure what kind of help to get," Beth explained to Rafe, "so I called your mother, and this is what we came up with."

"You two are obviously blessed by angels," Rafe said. "Bringing kids into this situation . . ."

"We knew it would turn out just fine," Pilar declared. "Those men needed the children to teach them a little about humanity and love."

A television reporter pressed forward into the crowd of ranchers, a cameraman beside him, video camera whirring. The reporter stuck a mike into Buddy Silver's face, and Buddy began trying vainly to explain that he and the others weren't actually "hunting down" the school's adopted wolf.

Silver was explaining that Julia had agreed to close the project when a young boy raced toward him, clearly unaware of Buddy's role earlier. "Daddy, Daddy, my school adopted Cochise!" he shouted proudly.

"Now if you'd like to expand what you just told me," the reporter said, not moving the mike away from Silver's mouth, even as the rancher's son squirmed between them.

"Well," Silver explained, looking very uncomfortable, "Miss Shelton told us . . ."

"Maybe I should speak for myself," Julia said, stepping forward.

"This is Julia Shelton," the reporter said into the mike, "head of the university's project. Is this the end of the hostilities, Dr. Shelton? Are you going to close down?"

"That was the idea ten minutes ago," Julia admitted, "but now, with all this community support, I doubt if I'd be *allowed* to move the wolves."

"But Mr. Silver said . . ." the reporter began again.

"If you would give us a few minutes, I believe Mr. Silver and I can come up with a statement for the media." Julia raised her voice so that Buddy Silver could hear, smiling when she saw his slight nod of agreement. She had never seen a man look so uncomfortable as Buddy Silver did just then, knee-deep in noisy, enthusiastic eight-year-olds, one of them his own son.

FIVE MINUTES LATER, Julia and Silver were ready to make their impromptu television and newspaper statement. The crowd gathered around, quiet for the first time.

Julia led off. "Several days ago there was a rumor that one of the range calves had been killed. Responding to that, my colleagues and I moved the wolves farther into the wilderness. Today another rumor surfaced, which resulted in a confrontation. As you can see, it has been resolved."

There was applause from the gathering, including a few of the cowboys, obviously egged on by their kids.

"However," Julia went on, "out of a spirit of community cooperation, we have agreed to move the wolves again, so there will be no possibility of another such rumor surfacing. Furthermore," she said with a smile, "Mr. Silver has offered to speak to the Cattlemen's Association about the possibility of donating funds, so that our project could purchase some of the land that we now lease. Beth Gilmer assures me that her father will back that decision."

There were additional cheers from the crowd.

Then a tight-lipped Buddy Silver had his moment. "Dr. Shelton has agreed to monitor her wolves to avoid any hunting of livestock. If a kill occurs, she has promised to pay for replacement at above market value."

There was polite applause, then someone called out, "Hey, let's see a handshake!"

Julia moved away from the television camera at last and fell into Jake's welcoming arms. "It's over," she exulted. "Somehow we all muddled through and it's over."

Jake kissed her thoroughly and looked into her dust-streaked face. Never had she seemed more beautiful. Never had he loved her more. "Oh, no, Julia, it's not over yet. There's a hell of a lot more to this story."

"And you're going to be around to see it unfold?" she asked.

"Be around? You bet I am. I'm here to stay, Julia."

"So am I, Jake," she said.

"Then I guess I'll be seeing you, Dr. Shelton."

"You can depend on it, Sheriff."

They heard the camera whir again, but Jake and Julia no longer cared what images it was capturing.

Epilogue

ONE YEAR LATER, Julia sat in her usual place at the computer. The wolves had adapted to their habitat, and a second monitoring station had been set up deeper in the desert, manned by her new assistant.

There'd been other changes in her life, as well. The den of the adobe house had been converted into a pink and white nursery for the most recent addition to the household. Elizabeth Forrester nestled against Julia's shoulder, wriggled slightly, then drifted off to sleep.

"Am I lucky, Lizbeth," Julia whispered, "to have you." The two-month-old had her mother's red hair, her father's green eyes and a wonderfully sunny and peaceful disposition.

Gently and rhythmically patting her baby's back, Julia watched the blips on the screen, smiling with sheer satisfaction. All of Sacajewea's cubs had survived and were thriving. Somehow the fledgling pack, drawing on eons of instincts, despite its many travails, had joined with Cochise and Sacajewea to rear the cubs. Against all odds, the project had succeeded in reintroducing the Mexican brown wolves into the wild.

Julia switched on the computer's data recorder and placed Elizabeth in the crib she kept in the office. She stood for a moment looking out the window, watching the night deepen and the clouds blow across the early-rising moon that hung low in the sky.

Jake slipped in the door. "Sorry to be late, but we had a city council meeting, and the sheriff's presence was required," he said with a grin. "But of all days to be late." He leaned over and kissed Julia. "Pilar said she'd babysit if we wanted to go out and celebrate our anniversary."

"I do want to celebrate, but at home," Julia said. "As long as Liz cooperates by staying asleep." She raised her face for one more kiss.

Jake obliged, then reached into his pocket. "Mail from California. Pilar passed it along. Rafe is still at the top of his grad school class, and Beth just got a raise at the newspaper. And yes, they both managed to survive Fred's visit."

"I'll read it later," Julia said. "I sure do miss them, though. The new assistant is very competent, but . . ."

"Not family like Beth and Rafe. They'll be home before Liz is walking." Jake went to the crib and ran his finger along the sleeping baby's cheek. "She is perfect, isn't she?"

Julia chuckled. "You ask me that ten times a day, and ten times a day I tell you that she's the most perfect thing in this often imperfect world."

"A world that's getting better all the time," he answered, taking her hand. "Come outside for a minute. I want to show you something."

They stood on the front porch and looked across the desert where the cactus was silhouetted against the darkening sky and stars were just beginning to twinkle. Julia remembered the first night they'd walked out there together. She'd compared him with the Big Bad Wolf, and he'd teased her good-naturedly. It seemed like only yesterday, though it was more than a year ago.

"A penny for your thoughts," he encouraged her.

"They're all about you, and they're all good."

"So are mine," Jake said. "I love it here, Julia. Once I thought it was lonely...."

"But it's not," she said. "It's magical and beautiful. What did you want to show me?"

"Just this," he said, gesturing to the scene before them. At that moment the clouds blew away and the full moon edged above the horizon to shimmer in the early-evening sky. "A lovers' moon, especially ordered for us."

They kissed, and in the fast darkening sky the moon rose slowly, majestically, bathing everything beneath it in a silvery sheen. From far away, floating on the wind, came the howl of a wolf. And then that lonely cry was joined by another and another until the desert air echoed with the sound—the music of the night.

Author's Note

In the United States, red and gray wolves have been successfully reintroduced into the wild. Mexican brown wolves are not so fortunate. There are fewer than fifty alive, all in captive breeding programs, awaiting their chance to be freed.

A Note From Madeline Harper

Each woman holds in her heart an ideal hero who has the ability to love, the strength to stand up for what is meaningful in life, and the courage to risk.

That's what my heroes are like. Jake Forrester isn't a perfect man, nor would he consider himself the heroic type. But when dangerous circumstances arise—saving a life in Vietnam or facing down an angry mob—Jake stands up for what he believes.

Jake also has to face the most difficult challenge of all—to be vulnerable with the woman he loves while remaining true to himself. To me, that is the true measure of a hero.

And let's not forget that there can never be a great hero without a great heroine! I hope you enjoy this special love story of Jake and Julia.

Books by Madeline Harper

HARLEQUIN TEMPTATION

HARLEQUIN Temptation

Rebels & Rogues

Jackson: Honesty was his policy...
and the price he demanded of the woman
he loved.

THE LAST HONEST MAN
by Leandra Logan
Temptation #393, May 1992

All men are not created equal. Some are
rough around the edges. Tough-minded but
tenderhearted. Incredibly sexy. The tempting
fulfillment of every woman's fantasy.

When it's time to fight for what they believe in,
to win that special woman, our Rebels and Rogues
are heroes at heart. Twelve Rebels and Rogues,
one each month in 1992, only from
Harlequin Temptation!

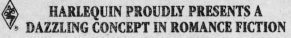

HARLEQUIN PROUDLY PRESENTS A
DAZZLING CONCEPT IN ROMANCE FICTION

One small town,
twelve terrific love stories.

TYLER—GREAT READING... GREAT SAVINGS... AND A FABULOUS FREE GIFT

Each book set in Tyler is a self-contained love story;
together, the twelve novels stitch the fabric of
the community.

By collecting proofs-of-purchase found in each Tyler
book, you can receive a fabulous gift, ABSOLUTELY
FREE! And use our special Tyler coupons to save on
your next Tyler book purchase.

Join us for the third Tyler book, WISCONSIN
WEDDING by Carla Neggers, available in May.

If you missed *Whirlwind* (March) or *Bright Hopes* (April) and would like to order them, send
your name, address, zip or postal code, along with a check or money order for $3.99 (please
do not send cash), plus 75¢ postage and handling ($1.00 in Canada) for each book ordered,
payable to Harlequin Reader Service to:

In the U.S.

3010 Walden Avenue
P.O. Box 1325
Buffalo, NY 14269-1325

In Canada

P.O. Box 609
Fort Erie, Ontario
L2A 5X3

Please specify book title(s) with your order.

Canadian residents add applicable federal and provincial taxes.

TYLER-3

Following the success of WITH THIS RING, Harlequin cordially invites you to enjoy the romance of the wedding season with

BARBARA BRETTON
RITA CLAY ESTRADA
SANDRA JAMES
DEBBIE MACOMBER

A collection of romantic stories that celebrate the joy, excitement, and mishaps of planning that special day by these four award-winning Harlequin authors.

Available in April at your favorite Harlequin retail outlets.

THTH

® **Harlequin**®

JANELLE TAYLOR

Valley of Fire

HARLEQUIN IS PROUD TO PRESENT *VALLEY OF FIRE* BY JANELLE TAYLOR—AUTHOR OF TWENTY-TWO BOOKS, INCLUDING SIX *NEW YORK TIMES* BESTSELLERS

VALLEY OF FIRE—the warm and passionate story of Kathy Alexander, a famous romance author, and Steven Winngate, entrepreneur and owner of the magazine that intended to expose the real Kathy "Brandy" Alexander to her fans.

Don't miss VALLEY OF FIRE, available in May.

FREE GIFT OFFER

To receive your free gift, send us the specified number of proofs-of-purchase from any specially marked Free Gift Offer Harlequin or Silhouette book with the Free Gift Certificate properly completed, plus a check or money order (do not send cash) to cover postage and handling payable to Harlequin/Silhouette Free Gift Promotion Offer. We will send you the specified gift.

FREE GIFT CERTIFICATE

ITEM	A. GOLD TONE EARRINGS	B. GOLD TONE BRACELET	C. GOLD TONE NECKLACE
# of proofs-of-purchase required	3	6	9
Postage and Handling	$1.75	$2.25	$2.75
Check one	☐	☐	☐

Name: _____

Address: _____

City: _____ State: _____ Zip Code: _____

Mail this certificate, specified number of proofs-of-purchase and a check or money order for postage and handling to: HARLEQUIN/SILHOUETTE FREE GIFT OFFER 1992, P.O. Box 9057, Buffalo, NY 14269-9057. Requests must be received by July 31, 1992.

PLUS—Every time you submit a completed certificate with the correct number of proofs-of-purchase, you are automatically entered in our MILLION DOLLAR SWEEPSTAKES! No purchase or obligation necessary to enter. See below for alternate means of entry and how to obtain complete sweepstakes rules.

MILLION DOLLAR SWEEPSTAKES
NO PURCHASE OR OBLIGATION NECESSARY TO ENTER

To enter, hand-print (mechanical reproductions are not acceptable) your name and address on a 3"×5" card and mail to Million Dollar Sweepstakes 6097, c/o either P.O. Box 9056, Buffalo, NY 14269-9056 or P.O. Box 621, Fort Erie, Ontario L2A 5X3. Limit: one entry per envelope. Entries must be sent via 1st-class mail. For eligibility, entries must be received no later than March 31, 1994. No liability is assumed for printing errors, lost, late or misdirected entries.

Sweepstakes is open to persons 18 years of age or older. All applicable laws and regulations apply. Sweepstakes offer void wherever prohibited by law. Prizewinners will be determined no later than May 1994. Chances of winning are determined by the number of entries distributed and received. For a copy of the Official Rules governing this sweepstakes offer, send a self-addressed, stamped envelope (WA residents need not affix return postage) to: Million Dollar Sweepstakes Rules, P.O. Box 4733, Blair, NE 68009.

✂ HT1U

ONE PROOF-OF-PURCHASE
To collect your fabulous FREE GIFT you must include the necessary FREE GIFT proofs-of-purchase with a properly completed offer certificate.

(See center insert for details)